PRAISE FOR CARNAGE ROAD

Jack Kerouac, Roger Zelazny and Cormac McCarthy have a new traveling companion. With *Carnage Road*, Greg Lamberson has taken his unique talent on a savage apocalyptic road trip tailor-made for the zombie generation. This book is dark gold, and demonstrates once again why readers who like their horror shot through with rock-n-roll and smart social commentary hold Greg Lamberson in such high regard.

> Joe McKinney, author of *Dead City*
> and *Apocalypse of the Dead*

PRAISE FOR GREGORY LAMBERSON

Gregory Lamberson is the sort of force that dark fantasy and horror are lucky to have. The multi-talented director of both the cult NYC backyard gorefest *Slime City* and its new sequel/remake *Slime City Massacre* genuinely loves what he does, expressing his rather unbalanced—and that's meant in the most positive way possible—psyche in as many media as he can get his mitts on.

> Chris Alexander, *Fangoria*

Filmmaker and author Greg Lamberson is one of the tireless creative minds that keep the horror genre vital whenever mainstream interest wanes.

> *Rue Morgue*

Greg Lamberson is the most cinematic author writing today...

> Bob Freeman, *The Occult Detective*

[Lamberson writes] truly dark horror fiction that will genuinely frighten even the well-seasoned horror reader, yet contains a knowing humor that contrasts well with the tension and scares.

> Norman Rubenstein, *Horror World*

ALSO BY GREGORY LAMBERSON:

Personal Demons: the Jake Helman Files
Desperate Souls: the Jake Helman Files
Cosmic Forces: the Jake Helman Files
Tortured Spirits: the Jake Helman Files
The Frenzy Way
The Frenzy War
Johnny Gruesome

N O N - F I C T I O N
Cheap Scares: Low Budget Horror Filmmakers Share Their Secrets

ALSO AVAILABLE NOW FROM PRINT IS DEAD BOOKS:

Pray to Stay Dead, Mason James Cole
World in Red, John Sebastian Gorumba
Scavengers, Nate Southard
Reanimated Americans, Martin Mundt
The Crossing, Joe McKinney
Dating in Dead World: The Collected Zombie Stories, Volume I, Joe McKinney

CARNAGE ROAD

GREGORY LAMBERSON

PRINT
IS
DEAD

NEW ORLEANS

2012

Carnage Road

First printing by Creeping Hemlock Press, April 2012

ISBN-10: 0-9847394-3-2
ISBN-13: 978-0-9847394-3-1

Cover photos by Kashfi Halford & Flavio Takemoto
Cover design & book design by Julia Sevin

A Print Is Dead book
Print Is Dead is a zombie-themed imprint of Creeping Hemlock Press
Editors: R.J. & Julia Sevin
Creeping Hemlock Productions, LLC

www.printisdead.com

www.creepinghemlock.com

Dedicated to John Russo,
creator of the ghouls

CARNAGE

Life is, in fact, a battle. Evil is insolent and strong; beauty enchanting, but rare; goodness very apt to be weak; wickedness to carry the day; imbeciles to be in great places, people of sense in small, and mankind generally unhappy. But the world as it stands is no illusion, no phantasm, no evil dream of a night; we wake up to it again for ever and ever; we can neither forget it nor deny it nor dispense with it.

Henry James

10

Thirteen of us rode down Sheridan Drive in Williamsville, heading in the direction of downtown Buffalo when coming from the Transit in Lockport. Our number had been twice as great before the dead rose; half of those no longer with us were killed and the other half left town with their families. Except for Boone, who handled a chopcycle, we all rode hogs: Harley Davidson two-wheelers. I'm not going to pretend that we were choir boys: the Floating Dragons had run drugs from Canada and guns from down south, anything to make a tax-free buck. We were "1%ers"—outlaw bikers, as opposed to the 99% of clubs that the American Motorcycle Association claimed were comprised of law-abiding citizens. Now we had one goal, as simple and instinctive as the ghouls' desire to eat human flesh: survival.

Deke was our leader, a hardcore biker who ruled the gang with a studded leather fist and put the good of the club above all else. His long dark hair and equally long gray beard framed his craggy face and inked biceps. Tasmara, Deke's old lady, had been bitten by a ghoul two weeks into the collapse. Deke perforated her brain before she had a chance to reanimate. His sons, Red and

Fixer, rode behind him, their loyalty unquestioning. But the death of their mother had turned both men sullen and Red had been on edge; the rest of us sensed his growing discontentment.

Weeds and Blowtorch served as Deke's chief lieutenants. Weeds had a rep for always being one step ahead in the game, any game, and for framing the big picture for a spot on the wall. But our picture had changed drastically, and the Dragons watched the world crumble around us. Blowtorch was Weeds's diametric opposite, a hotheaded killer with a clean-shaven dome and a handlebar mustache, like the strongman in a circus. No one messed with Blowtorch, and he kept everybody in line.

Boone and I rode in the middle of the procession, emblematic of our rank in the club. He was in his late twenties, blond-haired and blue-eyed, and I was thirty-six. We'd ridden together for ten years, and I guess you could say we were partners. My last name is Walker; my first name doesn't matter. I'm not as big as Blowtorch, but I'm big enough—6'1"—and I can be plenty mean when brought to a boil. I like to think I'm not quick-tempered, but a lot of people who have experienced my wrath would disagree.

Behind us, Comet drove our only cage, a pickup truck we'd boosted off of Military Avenue. Comet usually rode a hog but someone had to bring the truck for this mission. I smiled as wind resistance slapped my face. With the cherry tops gone there was no need to wear a brain bucket and I let my red hair trail me like flames from a torch and stayed in formation. We passed million-dollar mansions and Williamsville High School, where once upon a time, not so long ago, rich kids enjoyed private-school-quality education at a public school. Other than my fellow bikers, I saw no people or movement. Sheridan was a major street, but the populace had abandoned it.

None of us had any fender bunnies with us, and we were all packing. We'd always thought of ourselves as a secret army, and now the secret was out. I saw the long, tree-lined driveway to our destination: Wegmans, the super-sized supermarket. I leaned into my ape hangers and followed my brothers along the driveway, which led into a parking lot occupied by a half dozen cages.

My stomach tightened as we circled the lot: empty cages meant cagers inside the supermarket. Wegmans was a twenty-four-hour operation, but the martial law required them to shut down at night. No one should have been here at dawn, which meant citizens were looting the food we had come to take for ourselves. Probably staff members.

We circled the lot, and when Comet parked the truck we circled that in smaller rings. Deke pulled up front and swung one leg over the saddle of his bike. With his boots planted on the ground, Blowtorch pulled a pump action shotgun from his bike and used it to scan the windows like a pirate holding a spyglass. All around me, my brothers pulled rifles from leather holsters fastened to their steel mounts and raised them to their shoulders. I did the same with my Savage 110, which was ugly but efficient. With Red, Fixer, and Weeds at his side, Deke strode to the front doors and inspected them. Red shoved the metal frames, which didn't budge. The four bikers gestured at the doors and spoke in mild tones, like carpenters trying to solve a problem. Then they returned to our posse.

"The doors are locked," Deke said. "I guess that's gonna keep us out."

A smile came to my lips and I heard scattered laughter. Like I said, we were no choir boys.

Deke slid onto his saddle and said something I couldn't hear to Blowtorch, who nodded and holstered his shotgun. He started his bike, revved its engine, and took off, then circled us, gaining speed, and rocketed towards the doors. He popped a wheelie and charged the seam between the doors like a bull going after a matador, and the doors flew open.

Facing us, Deke threw a single fist at the sky. "As much as you can carry!"

Deke raced after B.T., who had disappeared inside, and the rest of us followed in single file. The supermarket was dark, and our headlights burned fake moonlight over boxes of Cocoa Puffs and Cheerios, the roar of our engines deafening. If you've never been inside a Wegmans, they're huge. This one must have had thirty checkout counters for the cashiers. I steered my bike along the wide aisle. The situation made me antsy: the headlights enabled us to see our loot, but they also allowed whoever else was in there to see us. Instant karma's gonna get you...

Riding around that store was like racing on an indoor track with the lights turned off. As we circled the perimeter, we broke off from the formation one by one and claimed our own aisle, circles of light dancing in the dark like UFOs around Devil's Tower. The power had gone off a week ago, so Weeds told us to forget about meat, dairy products, and other spoilable goods. I glided past shelves of canned soup and knew we had hit the jackpot. Back in the front of the store, I parked my bike in a checkout lane. With a foot-long flashlight in one hand, I located a shopping cart which rattled as I returned to my aisle. Why did

I always pick the one with the crippled front wheel?

It took me a while to find my way back to the canned soups. Bikes continued to roar and spit exhaust, accompanied by whoops and hollers. I'd lost track of Boone, but that was okay; we had each other's back, but we weren't joined at the hip like Siamese twins or anything. The gas fumes dissipated and the stench of rotten fruit and spoiled milk replaced them. Behind me, someone thought to pull down all the signs and banners from the front windows, admitting a lot more light through the grimy glass. I holstered my Colt and tucked the flashlight into the waistband of my jeans, and with eager hands tossed soup cans into the shopping cart two at a time. I figured we could live off Campbell's and Progresso for quite a while, so I filled the cart to the top, then wheeled it outside to the cage where Comet waited.

"All riiiiiiight," he said, a wide yellow smile appearing in the thick of his woolly beard. "Any trouble?"

"Not yet." Leaving him to pack the soup as the other brothers wheeled out their goods, I went back inside and pulled another shopping cart out of the lineup, this one with all four wheels in working condition. Where the hell were the citizens?

My brothers ran past me, their carts loaded with cases of beer, bags of potato chips, and packages of Hostess Twinkies. Clearly, they planned to party like it was 1999. I set off to find something at least partly nutritious and wound up in an unoccupied frozen foods aisle. Halfway up the aisle, I saw some frozen chicken wings, and it occurred to me I might never eat a Buffalo Wing again. Or a beef on weck, or a pizza sub, or any of the pounds-packing delicacies offered in Western New York. I stopped and glared at my dark reflection in the glass of the freezer display unit. Half out of curiosity and half out of blind optimism, I grabbed the handle and pulled the door open. No cold air seeped out, but the unit felt cool. Holding my flashlight in one hand, my fingertips brushed against the plastic bag of frozen wings and my mouth watered at the thought of Buffalo sauce.

A hand burst out from between the packages, knocking them aside, and seized my wrist. Its grip was colder than the chicken wings, and I screamed like a little girl. Aiming the flashlight at the back of the unit, I saw a pair of vacant eyes glaring out at me from the darkness. The pupils in the eyes did not dilate in the light. Another hand shot forward, clawing at my face, which I twisted away. The ghoul jerked me against the shelves and I smelled the rotting stench of death. With my gun hand clenched in its icy grip, I couldn't reach for my Colt .44, which I wore strapped to my right leg, so I flailed at the hand holding my wrist with the flashlight. One of the problems with ghouls is they feel no pain; you can break their bones and the fuckers won't even know it. All that my flashlight pounding accomplished was that my only light went out, so I couldn't see my attacker at all.

"Help!"

Somewhere in the supermarket—the cereal section, I think—a blood curdling scream answered. Another pair of hands burst through a selection of supposedly frozen fish sticks, and another pair burst through the chicken tenders near my knees: five hands besides the one already holding me, which amounted to twenty-four arthritic-looking fingers and half a dozen thumbs clawing the air around me. The lower hands grabbed behind my knees, and the irony dawned on me: we had gone grocery shopping at the mega grocery store, but I was about to be the main dish. Swinging the flashlight sideways, I heard the splitting of a skull, and the hand clutching my wrist released it. I dropped my right hand to the butt of my Colt and drew it from its holster just as the shape of a head emerged from beneath a shelf in front of my crotch. The ghoul pulled my knees against the shelf. I'm no homophobe, but as the dead thing's jaws snapped at my zipper, I felt an odd sense of relief when I realized that the crawling pile of pus had once been female. Sinking my butt closer to the floor, I jammed the long barrel of my revolver between two rows of teeth. The bitch worked her rotting lips over the barrel, and for a moment I could have sworn she thought it was my cock. Then she gnawed on the metal, which pissed me off, so I squeezed the trigger. The impact flung her back into the freezer and she released my knees. I fell ass-first to the floor, and as the freezer door swung shut I felt kind of stupid.

Gunshots erupted in other areas of the supermarket, and I knew we had a fight on our hands. No wonder we hadn't seen any of the citizens who had left their cages in the parking lot: they were all dead and unburied. Standing before the frozen Buffalo wings, I discerned the remaining four hands clawing at the closed doors. Packages of frozen food fell away, revealing the unblinking gazes of the ghouls inside. I shook my flashlight, but it was no use, so I tossed it aside and fanned the hammer of my Colt, gunfire shattering the glass. The hands disappeared like cockroaches on a kitchen counter when the lights are turned on, and my beloved Buffalo wings spilled out of a ruptured package and rained on the broken glass. Then the gun clicked in my hand.

I know what you're thinking: why the hell was I carrying a six-shooter during the apparent apocalypse? Because I liked it: I liked the feel of its pearl-handled grip and I liked the sound of its bark. But I'm not an idiot; I carry a custom-made speed-loader. Standing there in half darkness, I emptied the Colt's cylinder, and as I heard the empty shells scattering on the floor like marbles, I slammed in a fresh six-pack. Then an arm encircled my throat and I dropped the damned gun, and putrid breath misted the back of my neck. I turned in the thing's grip and slapped my one palm against its forehead just as its jaws snapped shut. Using both hands, I forced the thing back into the freezer, pressing it against the frozen pizzas and Hot Pockets. I slammed the door and pressed my weight against it.

"Help! I'm in Frozen Foods!"

I doubt anyone heard me over the bursts of gunfire, which sounded like firecrackers. The dead man in the freezer pounded against the glass door, and I looked down at the floor, where I saw the silhouette of my Colt. Releasing the door, I jumped sideways and scooped up the gun. What else could I do? The ghoul stepped out of the freezer as I dug into the pocket for my other speed load. As I slapped the fresh ammo into the Colt's cylinder, the man staggered toward me and I saw he wore a black work polo. It was too dark to read the name on his tag, which made me feel bad. I pressed the end of the barrel against his forehead and blew his brains all over the glass door. As he toppled to the floor, which he would never mop again, I heard someone moan behind me.

Jesus Christ, I remember thinking. *What now?*

Pivoting on one heel, I glimpsed four figures standing nearby. Where the hell were they all coming from? I managed to shoot one in the forehead before the other three charged at me. My heart jackhammered in my chest and I scrambled backward, forgetting about the dead pizza ghoul on the floor, which I tripped over. Landing on my back, I was careful not to drop my piece. As the three ghouls crouched over me, reaching for me with outstretched fingers like little kids at a barbecue, I raised my Colt and blew one of the silhouetted bastards off his feet. One of the remaining two grabbed my gun arm in both hands and pushed it to the floor, and the other one scrambled on top of me. They were working in tandem! Halos of light flashed behind their heads as twin explosions sounded. Soggy chunks of cold meat struck my face, and a moment later the ghouls pitched forward, collapsing on top of me, and stopped moving.

Have you ever been buried under two dead bodies that had just tried to make you their breakfast? It isn't pleasant. Ghouls stink worse than the most disgusting homeless person you've ever encountered. They evacuate their bowels at the time of death and don't bother to clean themselves. Gagging, I pushed one of the corpses off me. The other one seemed to levitate, then crashed into the freezer to my right. Boone stood over me, doubled over with laughter, a Beretta smoking in one hand. Sitting up, I shook my head.

"Very funny," I said, grateful the semi-darkness prevented him from seeing my face turn red.

"You and your damned cowboy gun!" he said between fits of laughter.

I got to my feet and wiped brains from my face.

"Cleanup in aisle seven!"

Despite the rhetoric offered by the Vatican and other religious institutions, and despite the criticism leveled at me and my administration by our political opponents, nothing on earth could have prepared us for this epidemic. We've lost contact with several military vessels that transporting our troops from the Middle East, and the troops remaining on our bases in Iraq, Afghanistan, Pakistan and Saudi Arabia are actively engaged in the same fight for survival we all face now. The personnel they already killed have risen up against them. Our great cities have already fallen: hospitals, police stations, and fire houses abandoned. The very threads of our society have come undone. My staff and I are evacuating to a safe location, where we hope to monitor the situation and provide what assistance and inspiration we can from afar. But without TV stations, telephone connections, or the internet, I fear this government can no longer serve you. My thoughts and prayers go out to every man, woman, and child watching or listening to this broadcast. Do what you can to preserve your communities, but above all else, do what you must to survive. Good luck, God bless you, and God bless the United States of America.

Final address of the final President of the United States

9

We lost two brothers on that shopping trip: Klemmer and Ox, neither of whom would be missed by anyone. Klemmer had been someone's prison bitch in Attica, and had pretty much acted like a weasel ever since his release. I worried that if he ever got pinched by the cherry tops he'd roll over on the rest of the Floating Dragons in half a heartbeat; I know I wasn't the only one who questioned his loyalty. He smelled bad, too. Ox was "as dumb as an ox," and he ate more than he earned and more than we could afford. I didn't wish either one of them ill, but if two of us had to go, it may as well have been them.

Much harder to take was seeing Deke with his left forearm wrapped in a bandage already spotting blood; a bag boy had bitten him in aisle ten, and I heard B.T. crushed the ghoul's head with his bare hands. In the parking lot, I saw B.T. and Weeds standing over Deke, who sat astride his bike, shaking his head in disbelief. I shook mine, too: Deke had been a great club leader, but no one survived the bite of a ghoul, and I wondered who would take his place at the head of the table. Red and Fixer had a certain amount of loyalty among the younger bikers, but they were too green to lead. A shared rule between Weeds and B.T. made the most sense since they had seniority, but how long could that last? Ego always gets in the way.

The mop-up operation went pretty easy. We found two ghouls in the room behind the butcher's counter and three more in the warehouse. We heard one clawing at the other side of the manager's office door, but decided it was too much trouble to break in and left the manager to starve forever. Fuck managers.

Sunlight poured into the supermarket. We didn't want to bother building a bonfire like those good old boys we saw on TV, so we left the ghouls wherever we had put them down. I filled my third shopping cart with canned fruits and vegetables, and turned a corner when I saw Hollywood marching a female ghoul in front of him. Despite his balding head and sagging eyelids, Hollywood was a young Turk anxious to ascend the club ranks without first paying his dues, a methhead with a ridiculous tuft of beard on his chin. We called him Hollywood because he had gone out west and come home telling tall tales about working as a stunt driver, but we all knew he'd only worked on a catering truck, serving lattes to people whose dreams had come true. He had cuffed the female ghoul's hands behind her back, and strapped a red gag ball inside her mouth. She had probably only been eighteen at the time of her death, a white gal with short dark hair. Even dead she appeared frightened. Knowing Hollywood, I didn't blame her.

"I hope you're going to wear protection," I said, not that I cared if he caught crabs or maggots.

Grinning with that arrogant look that I found so obnoxious, Hollywood showed me a box of extra-lubed condoms he had snagged from the pharmaceutical section. "I always double bag with these bitches."

Sick fuck. I was going to be pretty pissed off if the world gasped its last breath and this asshole was still around to see it.

We loaded the rest of our loot into the cage, and into the mini-trailer hitched to Boone's chopper, and we packed our saddle bags and backpacks, as much as we could possibly carry, and rode off.

The club house was located between Clarence and Lockport. Deke owned the property, not that deeds meant shit at the end of the world. A fence surrounded the double lot, good for keeping out ghouls even if we had to open the electric gate manually. Deke also owned the wrecking yard next door, which had doubled as a chop shop back when people still bought cars and parts. The club members spread out through the house, the garage, a barn, and the wrecking yard's garage and business office. It was a regular Spahn Ranch.

We had our share of mamas and fender bunnies, especially now that people needed each other to survive. I was unattached. I'd been seeing a cool lady who had a kid, but when things got bad, her ex—the kid's old man—took them to Kentucky, where his family members, a bunch of inbred survivalists, had built a compound they believed safe. I stepped aside because I didn't love her, and I didn't want to be responsible for her safety or her boy's.

Boone really liked a girl who was a straight up citizen and worked as a bank teller. Like a lot of people in Buffalo, her extended family all lived in the area; some of them had never even flown on an airplane. I don't know what went down when the time came to make choices, I only know that the chick's family disapproved of Boone's status as a Floating Dragon, and now she was nowhere to be seen. Boone is an easygoing guy, and if he was feeling pain he didn't show it. I guess we all had more important things to worry about than getting laid.

Thirteen of us went grocery shopping and eleven came back, one of us not long for this world. Ten little Indians. If this happened every time we needed supplies, the Dragons wouldn't be afloat for long. Nine women welcomed us back, and there were a few kids running around, too, which I didn't like; kids make you soft.

We left it to the women to unpack the supplies and organize them. Weeds suggested we keep everything under lock and key, and ration what we had, and Deke concurred, except for the beer: we all had a lot of frustration to burn off, and someone suggested we "pay tribute" to Klemmer and Ox even though no one gave a shit about them. What the hell, if the end of the world isn't a legit reason for a party, what is?

Someone fired up the generator so we could listen to tunes, which seemed like a waste of gas to me, and someone else set the fire pit ablaze. I spent a couple of hours in the barn, writing in this journal. I'd always wanted to be a writer when I was a kid. I was good in English and art, mediocre in history, and terrible at math and science. I knocked up a girlfriend senior year in high school and married her after graduation. Her father owned a garage and he hired me as an apprentice mechanic. I never attended college but I did my share of reading. The girl and me split up two years later. Her father didn't fire me, but I quit anyway and took a job at another garage. My ex remarried and the new guy took her and my son to Phoenix. I saw the boy a few times, then lost touch with him. I wonder if he went to college. If so, he had probably just graduated. Crazy.

Darkness settled and the booming tunes brought scores of ghouls to the fence. My biker brothers took turns shooting them with rifles, handguns, even arrows from a bow. I walked through the junkyard and found Boone sitting in a lawn chair in front of an old RV that wasn't good for anything.

"Where you been?" Boone offered me a beer.

Taking it, I sat in the empty seat beside him. "Just setting my thoughts down."

"Those must be some pretty deep thoughts."

I shrugged. "You seem mellow. Something got you down?"

"Ah, nothing important."

"Speak your mind." I saw he wanted to get something off his chest. "Go on."

"It's nothing big. I was just hoping to find something at the store, is all."

"Like what?"

Even before he answered, he looked like he felt foolish. "The magazine section was empty, and I was hoping to get the latest issue of *Spider-Man.*"

I stared at him. The world was coming undone and he was worried about Peter Parker. Fucking comic books, can you believe it? I wanted to smack him.

He must have seen the look in my eyes. "The last issue was a cliffhanger. I just want to know how the story ends."

Shaking my head, I dropped the issue of the issue.

"Look over there."

Following his gaze, I saw Weeds and Red deep in conversation over by the house.

"And over there."

Fixer and B.T. were having a similarly serious talk over by the barn. I didn't say anything, but this was not a good sign. Deke hadn't even passed yet, and alliances were forming over the leadership of the club; two factions I hadn't anticipated.

"What do you think?"

I popped the tab on my can, producing suds. "I think the world's going to the dogs."

"Yeah."

We drank our beer and listened to our brothers popping ghouls, the gunshots providing a surprising sense of calm. Hollywood sat shirtless on a chair at the other end of the RV. A woman named Baby Face who has Sunkist orange hair kneeled before him, blowing him. Baby Face was anything but; she had a nice set of silicone tits, but the face of a horse. Her head bounced up and down on Hollywood's joint, slurping away. She'd been a stripper at a titty bar up the Transit until the place was shut down for drugs, and somehow she had latched onto Hollywood. Her voice annoyed me, along with her Facebook lingo. The two of them were like carbon copies of each other, and if they ever procreated the human race was doomed.

"You don't want to know where that thing's been," I said, thinking of the ghoul Hollywood had raped.

Baby Face raised her head and Hollywood's flaccid little dick flopped against his leg like a dead little fish.

"WTF?" Baby Face said, wiping her mouth on one arm.

Hollywood glared at me. "Don't listen to grampaw, baby, just keep sucking."

I snorted. Hollywood was only twenty-nine, but he looked older than me, thanks to the crystal meth he loved so much. "Have you taken a good look at yourself lately?"

He jumped to his feet, causing Baby Face to fall over.

"OMG!" she said in that annoying voice of hers. "Who cares what some old guy says?"

I smiled. "Honey, I wouldn't let Deke catch you talking that way."

Hollywood huffed and puffed. "You're finished here."

"LOL," Baby Face said.

I don't know what irritated me more: the stupidity of Hollywood's threat, or the stupidity of his bitch. I nodded at his little dick. "Your threats are about as impressive as that pale little thing between your legs."

Hollywood charged at me with his thing flopping around, and I jumped out of my seat. I wasn't in any hurry to fight a methhead, but what the hell was I supposed to do? I struck him in the center of his chest, between his flabby man boobs, with the palm of my right hand. That's how you deal with drug addicts. His eyes went wide and he stutter stepped backwards, as I imagined his heart stuttered at that moment. Boone rose beside me but I held him back with one hand. I didn't need any help.

I didn't hear the gunshot because of the shots my brothers were firing at the ghouls, but I saw a third eye open in Hollywood's forehead, the red dot standing out even more because of his pallid skin. Hollywood's mouth opened and he narrowed his eyes, as if the dumb fuck wondered how I had managed to shoot him with no gun in my hand. Then he fell over with his little pecker hanging out.

"OMG! OMG! OMG!" Baby Face said beside him, but I didn't see any tears.

Boone seized my arm and pulled me towards the RV's missing door. Instead, I jerked him around the back of the camper, where we crouched between it and an old school bus half sunk into the ground.

"That camper's a death trap," I said.

"OMG! OMG! OMG!" Baby Face wailed out of sight.

"Should we get her?" Boone said.

"Nah, maybe they'll put her out of our misery."

We heard gunfire, a lot of it. Machine guns. Bullets ripped into the camper's metal walls and shattered its windows. The gunshots stopped, and I knew a lot of our boys were down.

"This is the police," a voice said over a megaphone. "We have the entire property surrounded."

Boone and I exchanged glances. No way in hell was the property surrounded.

"Lower your weapons and admit us onto the grounds."

Random rifle shots responded, and machine guns responded to them. A series of soft explosions prefaced white smoke spreading out above the ground.

"Lockport cops, Clarence, or Amherst?" Boone said, drawing his Beretta.

"Maybe all three."

"What do you think they want?"

"All that food we took today, all our guns, our bikes, and probably the women."

"I take it you don't think they plan to arrest us."

"Arrest us for what? The government's down. There are no laws."

"Then I can't get the chair for killing a cop?"

"There are no cops, either. That's a private army, just like we are. Only a fool would take prisoners."

Boone ran to the front of the RV and peeked around the corner. "A bunch of our guys are down and not moving."

Drawing my Colt, I felt ridiculous. "We need better ordinance. Let's get to the barn or our bikes."

"How the hell are we going to do that?"

I watched the clouds of tear gas spreading over the property. Then I took off my shirt. "Close your eyes and hold your shirt over your nose and mouth."

"Are you crazy? How are we going to see where we're going? And if we reach the barn, our own people will probably shoot us by mistake."

"Then I guess it's got to be the bikes. They're two-hundred yards ahead. The gas is about to envelop us anyway."

"Shit."

I waited for the gas to obscure everything between us and the street, then sprinted forward. I knew the terrain well, but it's hard to run blind and hold your breath at the same time. I heard Boone's footsteps behind me. When the ground turned hard, I knew we'd reached the parking area. Now we just had to find our bikes with our eyes closed. Somewhere ahead an engine roared, and then I heard the gate smashing open as a large vehicle careened in our direction. I found a bike but had no idea if it was mine. It didn't matter: we all had rifles mounted on our hogs now and I pulled one free of its holster.

"Got one!" I said, trying not to breathe.

Too late: my lungs, nasal passages, and eyes caught fire.

"Fuck this!" I heard Boone draw a rifle from another bike.

Feeling the front wheel of a Harley, I knew which direction we would find the house. "This way!"

With my lungs searing, I ran. I heard machine-gun fire coming from up above me, and remembered that Deke kept an AK-47 in his room. Shots rang out around us, and it was hard to tell which side fired which weapons. The gas cleared and I saw the house, not to mention the Remington in my hands. I sprinted for the nearest corner and ducked around it, gasping for breath. Boone joined me just seconds later. We hacked and coughed and spat and cried, like real men.

"Should we go inside?" Boone said.

"No, we'll be trapped in there. Let's see what's around the corner."

As we rounded the back of the house we saw a cherry top parked perpendicular to the barn, with two cops firing shotguns from behind it. I never thought I'd shoot a man in the back, much less a former cop, but you'd be surprised what you're willing to do when your back's against the wall and your life's on the line. I raised the Remington to my shoulder, aimed, and fired. I took out one cherry picker and Boone took out the other. The next corner provided us with a view of vehicle that resembled a UPS truck except for the letters SWAT stenciled on the side in military script.

Rounds ricocheted off the vehicle, fired from multiple windows of the house, sparks flying in all directions. Our brothers in the barn opened fire since they were no longer under siege. Two men in SWAT uniforms emerged from behind the truck, running towards us, followed by two more. Having no choice, we opened fire. The cherry pickers wore bulletproof vests, so we didn't kill them, but we drove them back where they'd come from and heavier fire pinned them down. Soon the shooting stopped.

So goodbye, Yellow Brick Road...

Sir Elton John

8

When the smoke cleared, we realized how much trouble we were in: Red and Fixer, Weeds and Blowtorch had all been killed, effectively wiping out the line club's line of succession. Counting Hollywood, Klemmer and Ox, we had lost half our membership in a single day. We found the bodies of eight dead ex-cops, and according to Deke, two cherry tops had driven off when the tide of battle had changed. Three of our women had been killed too. I don't think I'd ever screwed any of them.

Deke had fought hardcore, firing his AK-47 from his second floor window like a gangster in an old black-and-white crime drama. He'd gone through three clips by the time Boone and I turned things around.

The rest of us had ugly work ahead of us: thirteen men had been killed on the property, including our five brothers. They were down, but they weren't out. We dragged their bodies and laid them side by side on the grass, then circled them like a Polish firing squad. The wind blew and crickets chirped, and an hour passed.

"I gotta take a leak," Hartke said, heading towards the barn.

On the ground, one hand of a dead cop twitched. A leg went spastic. Boone took out his Beretta and capped the rising ghoul twice in the head, Mafia style. The corpse stayed dead. And so it went, body by body, making sure the dead stayed that way.

Besides me and Boone, three men remained standing: Comet, Hartke, and

Anderson. I didn't count Deke, because he was no longer standing; after exerting himself in the firefight, he had collapsed in bed, pale faced and ridden with fever. Time was running out for him. Hartke and Anderson were pards like me and Boone, and each man had his own lady. Between the four of them, they had most of the kids, too.

"Should we bury them?" Comet said over the sound of the generator after we finished shooting the dead men.

"Fuck no," Boone said. "Just drag them into the fire pit."

"That will smell awful."

"They're dead. They're going to stink no matter what. We have to do something about that gate before we can even think of sleeping. I'll be damned if I'm going to exhaust myself digging graves, too. It's a brave new world, boys: the dead are everywhere. What difference does it make if we bury these guys?"

"Five of them are our brothers," Hartke said. "And three of them were our sisters. It's about respect."

Boone spat. "Respect? As in, 'respect the dead'? Do the dead respect us? Hell, no! They eat us. Let them rot, or let them burn."

No one argued further.

"The ones who got away are probably joining up with others at a pigpen now," I said. "They'll be back."

Boone gave me a serious look. "I bet they're holed up in Orchard Park. That station's underground, real high tech."

Sometimes Boone surprised me, not that he was dumb or anything. "You're right."

"That gate's all smashed up," Comet said.

"Find the keys for that SWAT truck and park it there. Bring out all the guns and ammo, then lock the doors and keep the keys with you."

"Right."

I walked to the house, its siding freckled with bullet holes. Inside, wood chips, plaster dust, and broken glass covered everything. A lot of the canned goods from Wegmans had been ruptured. My feet crunched broken glass, and my anger rose. I had been coming here for years—over a decade!—and had even lived here. I felt violated.

I made way upstairs to Deke's room. He had left the light on, and two women, Jewel and Denise, played nurse. They were busy cleaning broken glass off the floor. Through the broken window, I heard Comet driving the SWAT truck around on the lawn. Looking at Deke, I had to wonder if he had already died: not only had his flesh turned milky white, but his eyes appeared sunken, his cheeks drawn in—and Deke was not a skinny man, by any means. He opened his eyes when I sat on the edge of the bed, and with visible effort he swallowed.

"How'd we do?" Deke's voice sounded hoarse.

"We kicked ass, what do you think?"

"Any survivors besides the pigs in those two cherry tops that got away?"

I shook my head. "Every one of them that came onto the property is dead."

"They'll be back. They can't just let something like this go."

"I know."

He nodded at the women. "What aren't these two telling me? Where are my boys?"

I hesitated, but he must have seen the answer in my eyes, because his watered up.

"What about Weeds and B.T.?"

I shook my head and he let out a tremulous sigh. In that moment, he seemed to age ten years.

"You've got seniority then."

"No. Comet is older than me, and he's been with the club longer."

Deke's expression hardened, the old ferocity returning to his eyes. "You listen to me. Comet ain't all there upstairs. You've got to lead what I built. Promise me you won't let it fall apart."

I gazed into desperate, fading eyes. "I promise."

When I went outside I found Hartke and Anderson sitting on the porch with shotguns in their laps and M-16s piled at their feet.

"How many of those did you find?" I said.

"Six," Hartke said.

"I'll take one for myself and one for Boone."

"Boone already took one for himself, and one for you."

"Ammo?"

"There was a case full of clips. He took your share."

"Where is he now?"

"He's in the barn. We said we'd take first watch."

Across the yard, I saw the dim glow of lanterns coming from the barn where Boone and I stayed. The women and children had moved into the house. "Turn off the generator soon, will you?"

I didn't want to give Comet orders. For one thing, Deke was still alive. For another, Comet knew he held seniority over me. Tension hung in the air between us. Then he smiled.

"Just as soon as everyone's settled down inside."

I found Boone in the barn, lying on his back with one leg crossed over the other and one arm shielding his eyes from the lanterns' soft glow.

"You think they'll be back tonight?" he said.

I sat on my mattress and pulled off my boots. "Nah, they'll want to reconnoiter when the sun comes up, see how many of us are left and how able bodied we are. Maybe they'll even hit back in the daytime."

"You gonna be the new boss man?"

I lied down. "That's what Deke says."

"There's women and children to watch out for, and not a whole lot of men."

"Just what I want. We'll find others."

"Maybe."

A minute later, he snored. I was too tired to get up and turn down the lanterns, so I just closed my eyes and let them burn.

I woke to the sound of a car door shutting and jumped to my feet. Comet, Hartke, and Anderson stood around the truck. Sally, who had been Red's girl, sat behind the cage's wheel with two other women beside her. I saw the heads and shoulders of kids sitting in the truck's bed. The sun had only just risen, and the guys had rolled their bikes over to the cage.

"What is it?" Boone said behind me.

"You'd better get up." I left the barn and crossed the yard barefoot. The morning light revealed grass torn up by gunfire, and smoke from the fire pit wafted through the air. The stench made me gag.

"Good morning," Anderson said, just to make sure everyone else saw me coming.

"What's going on?"

Comet offered a weak attempt at a smile. "We don't think it's a good idea to stick around. Those cops could be back any time, and there's going to be a lot more of them this time."

I heard Boone's footsteps behind me. He'd taken the time to pull on his boots. "So you're just going to leave Deke here?"

Sitting in the front seat, Jules and Denise averted their eyes.

"Deacon's not going to last the day," Comet said. "Is it worth getting killed over just to watch him die?"

I held his gaze. Beside me, Boone said nothing.

"You could come with us. You *should* come with us."

I felt my jaw tightening. I don't know why I ever expect people to show any loyalty. "I don't think so."

"Boone? We got plenty of women to go around."

"Deke led the Dragons for twenty years. It isn't right to run out on him. I'm staying with Walker."

"Good luck to you both, then."

Comet walked over to his bike and climbed onto it. A moment later, Baby Face ran around the other side of the truck, where she must have been hiding so we wouldn't see her. She hopped onto the back of Comet's bike and wrapped her arms around him. She didn't appear to be too broken up about Hollywood. I guess some people just recover from trauma faster than others. Comet looked over his shoulder at me and winked, then kickstarted his bike, which revved to life.

Boone walked to the back of the truck and patted its gate and waved to the kids. He was a lot softer than me. "You all take care of yourselves, now. Be good and listen to the grownups. Don't go wandering off."

Hartke and Anderson mounted their bikes with their women behind them. Comet took off first, followed by the cage, and then Hartke and Anderson. As the truck rolled out, I saw the kids had been packed in with luggage and supplies, which reminded me of *The Grapes of Wrath* and *The Beverly Hillbillies*. As the mini-caravan drove off, Boone rejoined me.

"So much for the burden of leadership," he said.

"Fuck it," I said. But I hoped they would all be okay. Well, maybe not Baby Face.

We ate soup and canned corn for lunch, and washed it down with warm beer. I sat with Deke while Boone watched for the cops from the front porch. If they were watching us, they knew we were severely undermanned. Deke sucked in air with a loud, protracted gasp and let it out. His breathing grew shallow, and a death rattle escaped from his lips. He looked at me with unblinking eyes and I set them with my fingers. It felt strange to be sitting in that room with the cooling corpse of a man I'd known almost half my life. With no sense of urgency, I walked over to the shattered window and called Boone's name. He stepped into view a moment later, squinting at me with one eye.

"Deke's gone. Why don't you dig him a grave right there, so you can still keep an eye on the road?"

He scrunched up his face. "Are you serious?"

"Yeah."

Without complaining, he set off for the barn to find a shovel. I looked over at Deke and wondered how long it would take for him to rise. I pulled the sheet over his head and sat in the rocking chair with my Colt in my lap. The shadows in the room stretched and narrowed.

"Walker!"

I went to the window. Boone stood next to a fresh grave, resting his weight on the shovel.

"I'll be down in a bit. Why don't you pack some food for a road trip?"

Tossing the shovel aside, Boone entered the house. When I turned around, I faced a ghost, and my heart leapt in my chest: Deke had risen, his head and body still covered by the sheet. Moving forward, I set the barrel of the Colt against his head and squeezed the trigger, splattering the back wall with his brain. The body fell back, the sheet coming loose, and I gazed at Deke's dead features. His eyes had opened again.

I heard Boone taking the stairs two at a time, and he ran through the open doorway and looked at Deke. We exchanged glances.

"How do we get him downstairs?" Boone said.

"I guess we carry him."

Boone pondered this. "Why don't we just throw him out the window? It's already broken."

I stared at him. "We stayed here all day, waiting for him to die and come back. We risked our lives to bury him because he was the leader of the club.

It seems wrong to just throw him out the window like some piece of broken furniture."

Boone shrugged. "He's dead twice over. He won't feel any pain."

I looked through the door at the narrow stairway. Deke was a big man with a classically heavy biker build. Then I glanced at the window space. "What the hell."

Groaning, we lifted him out of bed and half carried him, half dragged him to the window. Catching our breath, we shoved him out and watched the body plummet to the ground, where it missed the grave by about a foot. Deke's neck snapped and one arm flopped into the hole.

"Damn," I said. "We almost got him in."

"What are you going to do? We tried."

Boone was right: throwing Deke out the window was a hell of a lot easier than carrying him down the stairs would have been.

After we packed Deke in dirt, we also packed what belongings we could, not that either one of us owned much. I shoved handguns and ammo into one saddlebag and food into the other. Reluctantly admitting that the Colt wasn't going to cut it out in the wild, I holstered a .45 in its place, but I saved the six-shooter for sentimental reasons. It had served me well.

We stowed the M-16s, ammo, and canned food in the mini-trailer attached to Boone's chopper and put on our matching wraparound shades.

"Where do you want to go?" Boone said.

I considered the question. "How about Canada?"

"Canada? What the hell's in Canada?"

"Exactly. There's hardly any people there compared to here. Fewer people means fewer ghouls."

I could see by the look in his eyes that Boone didn't like the idea. "I don't know, man. I like America."

"Both countries are North American," I said, trying to reason him.

"I don't mean continents, I mean countries. I'm an American."

I smiled. "Yes, you are."

"Besides, Canada's as cold as Buffalo. I've been cold my whole life. I want to go somewhere warm."

"All right, where do you want to go?"

"I've been thinking about Hollywood."

"What are you thinking about him for?"

"Not him. I stopped thinking about that asshole before his body hit the ground. The place, Hollywood! I've never been there."

I blinked at him. "Hollywood's in California. That's all the way on the other side of the country."

"So? We've got no responsibilities, no runs to make. Let's take a real road trip and see America."

I shook my head. "You're crazy..."

"Come on, man! Let's get the hell out of New York before winter comes."

"If you only want to beat the cold, let's just go to Florida. Then we'll still be on the East coast."

"I don't want to go to Florida. I've been to Florida. I want to go someplace I've never seen before. Besides, something tells me Disney isn't very fun anymore."

Passion confounds me. "Hollywood. What the hell are we going to do in Hollywood?"

"What the hell are we going to do here? Let's just go. We'll lie on the beach and look for movie stars. What we do there isn't important. Getting there is. We'll be like pioneers."

I raised my hands in surrender. "All right. Jesus Christ, let's go find America."

Though the world may mock Peter Parker, the timid teenager... it will soon marvel at the awesome might of... Spider-Man!

Amazing Fantasy #15

7

I wanted to start early in the morning, but we knew we had to leave the club house far behind as soon as possible. We moved the SWAT truck out of the gate space, kicked our bikes to life, and hit the open road. It felt strange traveling familiar roads we knew we'd never see again, and yet liberating, too. We were the last of the Floating Dragons, and we knew it. Comet, Hartke, and Anderson no longer counted, riding escort for a cage full of women and children. I didn't fault them for their humanity—society's got to survive somehow—but a true 1%er had to be free, not anchored to a pickup truck full of saltines and Pampers. I weaved my Harley from one side of the road to the other, whooping and hollering as if I'd never been free before.

I weaved my Harley from one side of the road to the other, whooping and hollering as if I'd never been free before. Maybe I hadn't: married at a young age, tied to a job... even in the club, I basically served Deke. I never thought I'd run drugs or guns, but I came to view the kilos of cocaine and the Glocks in their boxes like any other commercial product.

Between the three wheels on his chopper and the mini-trailer behind him, Boone didn't get to enjoy our newfound status to the degree I did, but he seemed happy enough whenever we made a pit stop. We soon learned that even the simple, natural act of taking a leak had become a two-man operation: one to piss, and the other to cover him with a rifle. I didn't plan to jerk off anytime soon.

A sign for Interstate 90 appeared ahead, and I heard Boone honking the horn on his chopper. When I checked my rearview mirror I saw him waving for me to turn left. A few families loitered in yards, their expressions pensive as we passed them, and some ghouls staggered around without much direction. One burning house made for a creepy sight because no people stood gawking at it. As we moved into more unfamiliar territory, I found it hard to tell if the occasional wreck we spotted in the street was the result of a recent accident, or if the damaged vehicle had simply been left to rot.

We took I-90 West past Dunkirk and Fredonia into Pennsylvania, and made the mistake of getting off in Erie. The city made Buffalo look like an urban paradise even before the fall, and now things appeared far worse. Overturned cars burned on Peach Street, spewing black smoke into the sky while a fire horn blared unanswered. Flames licked out of the windows of a tall hotel. Citizens ran in every direction, smashing windows, looting, and beating each other. Cherry tops were nowhere to be seen, and the slower-moving ghouls did little more than observe the chaos. Bodies lay on the bloody asphalt, and I wondered how long they would stay there. A woman screamed in pain to my left, and a child cried in terror to my right. A siren wailed from a motionless fire engine, its strobes splashing crimson light on the ghouls who feasted on firefighters. A man charged in front of me, less frightened of my bike than the ghouls pursuing him. I weaved between the predators and their prey, Boone close behind me.

A sign for I-90 loomed ahead and Boone honked his horn again. Looking into my rearview mirror, I saw him waving for me to get on the ramp. Nodding, I complied. I guess we'd both had enough of Erie. We followed the highway deeper into PA, careful to avoid Pittsburgh. You had to be crazy to go there, after everything that had happened.

The first stories had came out of the Steel City: reports of lunatics running wild in the suburbs and more rural areas of Pennsylvania, biting anyone they could lay their jaws on, trying to eat them alive. The next day, the unprovoked attacks spread into the city, causing a panic. Police in riot gear responding to the emergency calls fired rubber bullets into a crowd of apparently deranged individuals. After the first three officers fell, their comrades switched to real ammunition. Three more officers died before the remaining police discovered that only well aimed headshots brought down the lunatics. Half a dozen officers who suffered bites were hospitalized. Then came the news that the initial victims had risen, only to attack those around them as they had been attacked. The fallen police rose as well.

The media ate it up, with cable news stations anxious to spread the word, and the terror, to juice up their ratings. The first proclamation that the dead were rising came from FOX News, which decreed the "uprising" a socialist plot. By dusk, the mayor of Pittsburgh declared martial law, and by nightfall MSNBC and CNN reported that similar attacks were occurring in Washington, D.C., Chicago, and Louisiana. Within hours, all of the news outlets broadcast graphics resembling election night results, only all 50 states had turned red. Reports came in from Afghanistan, Pakistan, Iraq, Paris, Italy, Argentina, Mexico City, and Japan. If the public needed convincing that the situation had become grave, the networks made the point by preempting their late night talk shows. Instead, talking heads debated the cause of the global emergency: a fallen communications satellite had spread radiation or alien spores; a secret military experiment had gotten out of control, infecting the world with a man-made virus; a Biblical plague was paving the way for the return of Jesus Christ; and the President himself was the Antichrist.

By morning, governors across the United States declared statewide emergencies. In Washington, D.C., the President's spokesperson told reporters, "We can confirm that the recently deceased are rising, and are exhibiting signs of cannibalism. The President is working closely with state leaders to address this crisis, and will issue a statement soon. The priority now is that people don't panic. Stay home when possible, or travel to work in groups. Follow the instructions and protocol established by your local authorities."

Irate citizens formed militias and searched houses door to door for the undead. Ghouls were shot in the brain, bodies burned in bonfires. Thousands of people had been killed overnight in the U.S., and many of them refused to stay dead. News anchors announced that the bite of a ghoul caused swift death and resurrection. With the U.S. engaged in four different wars, most military personnel were stationed on foreign soil, and most of the National Guard had been dispatched overseas to offer support. Within three days, the protests started: the very people who wanted big government out of their lives suddenly wanted that same government to protect them from this new threat within the country's borders. The President ordered an immediate withdrawal of U.S. troops from the Middle East, only to learn that the first troops would not return for a month. By then, it would be too late.

One week into the Crisis on Finite Earth, Hollywood shut down production of all TV shows and movies. Two weeks into the crisis, all businesses deemed nonessential were ordered closed. Three weeks in, nationwide riots began, and community organizers fought to hold the fabric of society together; newspapers ceased publication. During the fourth week, cable news channels stopped broadcasting. Local stations remained on air as long as volunteers ran them. Then the looting began, and Deke decided the Floating Dragons needed groceries.

Entering Ohio, we cut between Akron and Cleveland. "Finding America" didn't mean finding cities overrun with ghouls. We drove along flat roads surrounded by withered crops, and as the sky darkened, ghouls staggered around the fields like scarecrows come to life. One thing was certain: we sure as hell couldn't sleep out in the open. We needed to find protected shelter, or we'd have to ride all night... and we didn't really have enough gas for that.

Half an hour after I switched on my headlight, I saw a small farmhouse -outside, peering in. When we slowed at the driveway, several of them rotated their heads in our direction. The fence had been threaded with barbed wire, broken glass, and strips of wood with nails sticking out. I pulled my Savage 110 from its holster and aimed it at the ghouls while Boone raised high-powered binoculars equipped with night vision to his baby blues. Several more ghouls turned in our direction. I wanted to shout something sarcastic at my partner, but I didn't want to make the damned dead things any more curious about us.

"There's someone up there on the porch," Boone said. "Some old guy sitting in a rocking chair, holding a rifle."

A few ghouls separated from the pack and headed toward us. I sighted in on one and blew his forehead out. The dead farmer weaved from side to side for a moment, and I feared he was going to square dance. Instead he fell face down into the tall grass, which did nothing to deter his undead companions. I aimed at a skinny dead girl who couldn't have been more than sixteen. The rifle spat a muzzle flash that resembled a bouquet of lilies, but the round missed its target. I fired again and missed again.

"Shit."

Boone pulled out his rifle and raised it to his shoulder. I didn't intend to let the little fucker save my ass again, so I fired first, taking out the little lady's right eyeball. Her left eye zeroed in on me, and she shucked and jived in my direction—until Boone relieved her head of future aches by sending her brain to home plate. She fell backwards and disappeared.

"Showoff," I said.

All of the ghouls came for us. Some staggered into the dirt driveway, hindering our view of the front gate.

"Who goes there?" a deep voice said over a speaker mounted atop the gate. "Friends or foes?"

Boone and I traded puzzled expressions.

"Friends!" we said in unison.

"Well be quick about it." A lock buzzed and the gates swung inward.

He didn't have to tell us twice. I gunned my bike and raced through the opening. A bear of a man walked down the hill from the farmhouse. He carried a lantern in one hand, a rifle leaning against one shoulder. As I pulled over to him, he handed the lantern to me and lowered his rife. With Boone pulling up beside me, I looked over my shoulder: the gate had already started closing, but three ghouls had gotten inside the compound. Three rifle shots later, they lay on the ground. Once we killed our engines, I heard the steady chug-chug of a generator. The man—who must have stood 6'4" and had thick iron-gray hair parted at one side, and a full beard—picked took back his lantern and strode toward the unmoving ghouls. As he passed me, I noticed a clerical collar. Boone stood and stretched, and our host spoke. I wondered who the hell he was talking to over there, then realized he was praying. When he had finished, he walked back to us.

"I never saw anyone pray for those things before," Boone said.

"No soul on earth is more wretched than theirs are." The man gestured at the three corpses on his front lawn. "Now they're free. Where are you boys heading?"

"Hollywood," I said, feeling foolish. "I'm Walker, and this is Boone."

"I'm Jorge. I'd shake your hands, but mine are full. You two want to be movie stars?"

"I just want to see the West Coast," Boone said.

"Well, you're welcome to stay the night. You'll have to share a room, though. I stay up late in the living room."

"That's nothing we haven't done before. We're used to each other's snoring."

"Bring your machines up to the house, then."

As Boone sank into the saddle of his chopper, I glanced at the ghouls on the other side of the fence. They still wanted in, even though they saw what had happened to their fellows.

We sat in Jorge's kitchen, eating his soup and drinking his whiskey. The lights flickered occasionally, and a radio offered low static.

"Where you from?" our host said.

"Buffalo," Boone said.

Jorge aimed a spoon at the patches on my jacket. "You belonged to a club?"

"The Floating Dragons."

"Where's the rest of your outfit?"

"Most are dead. A few set off for paradise."

"Why didn't you go with them?"

I shrugged. "There's no such thing."

"Maybe not in this world." He lit a cigarette and exhaled smoke. "Sorry, I'd offer to share, but when my supply is gone, that's it. I pity those poor ghouls then."

"Why are you still here?" Boone said. "It looks like all of your neighbors cleared out."

"My neighbors are outside, trying to come in and eat me. They're why I'm still here: they're my flock."

"You just shot three of them," I said.

"Hey, I don't have all the answers, man. I'm as confused and conflicted as the next guy. Are your souls more deserving of protection just because you're alive and they're not? I have to go with 'yes.' I'm sick of ghouls, they're all the same, with just one thing on their mind: eating the living. Jesus Christ, that doesn't make for interesting repartee or interesting sermons. It isn't very fucking intellectual, you know what I mean? I just know that they need me, and God put me right here, right now, for a reason. So I'll tend to my loathsome flock while their souls are in those rotting shells, and when the time comes, I'll do my part to send them on their way."

"Why don't you just kill them all and send them all on their way now? Then you'd be free to go somewhere safe."

"There is no safe place. But I hear what you're saying, and I'm wrestling with different scenarios. Hopefully God will provide me with an answer."

"Do you think so?"

"I'm afraid he already has." He said this with good cheer and then stood. "How about some coffee?"

"I'd love some," I said.

"Me too," Boone said. "I miss Tim Horton's more than I can say."

Jorge filled three mugs with steaming coffee. "I'm Cuban. This is way stronger than that drive-thru sludge." He set the mugs before us and set out a carton of non-dairy creamer. "Sorry, I ran out of creamers."

We poured the powder into our coffee and waited for it to cool.

"I imagine I will kill them all eventually. But then others will come, and I'll have a new flock. It seems like a neverending proposition. I see myself dying here, and being stuck inside this compound alone, trying to get out, while they're all out there, trying to get in. I'll be the loneliest ghoul in the class."

"Blow your brains out," Boone said. "Then you can't come back."

Tapping his collar, Jorge smiled. "I can't do that. I may just be a country preacher, but my faith is still my faith."

"What denomination are you?" I said.

"Does it matter? Really, there are no religions left. Maybe that's a good thing. No more religious differences means no more wars, just the living and the non-living."

I sipped his coffee and my brain perked right up. "That's strong enough to raise the dead."

Jorge raised his hands. "Not guilty."

We relocated to the living room, where Jorge lit another cigarette. He wasn't making much of an effort to ration his supply. Riffling through magazines on the coffee table, Boone froze with a rapturous look on his face. He held a comic book in his hands like a delicate piece of glass art.

"Holy shit, *Spider-Man* #999!" He looked up at me with an astonished expression. "This is the one I've been looking for!"

"Take it, it's yours," Jorge said, enjoying his tobacco.

Boone looked as if he was being born again. "Really? Are you serious?"

Jorge waved him off. "Yeah, sure. I just picked it up for the kids, not that there are any living ones around here to appreciate it now."

We took one of the lanterns into the first floor bedroom, where we at least had twin beds. I shed my clothes like a grimy second skin and climbed under the covers nude. The mattress felt soft, and I folded my arms behind my head and closed my eyes. Boone moved the lantern close to him so he could see his comic book, and I listened to him turning the pages. Fifteen minutes later, the room turned dark and quiet.

"How was your comic?" I said.

"It was all right, I guess." I heard the disappointment in his voice.

"You didn't like it?"

"No, it was good."

"What, then?"

"It was 'to be continued.'"

I don't remember dreaming, and when I awoke I saw that Boone had left his bed. I found him taking a bath in an old cast-iron tub in the back yard that was heated by a fire beneath it. A joint dangled from his mouth.

"Wash up," my partner in crime said. "Who knows when we'll get the chance again."

I trained my eyes on a dozen chickens I saw in a coop fifty feet away. After my bath, and after Jorge served us scrambled eggs, we spread our maps across the kitchen table. Jorge ran one finger across the map.

"We're here. Follow this highway into Indiana. You want to avoid these points"—he indicated a triangle—"because there are state police stations there. I heard a lot of cops have banded together and formed private armies. You don't want to mess with them. There are a number of reservations there; maybe you can get gas."

I doubted anyone would share gas now that no one was producing it, but I thanked him anyway. He walked us to our bikes.

"Thanks for the hospitality," I said.

"Thanks for the company. It's nice to talk to people who can answer."

We started our engines. Raising his rifle to one shoulder, Jorge triggered the gates, which swung open, and we took off. I glimpsed ghouls on either side of us and heard a gunshot. Then we returned to the road.

I'm goin' back to Indiana…

The Jackson 5ive cartoon

6

It rained in Indiana. Riding our bikes through the mud, we discovered a dilapidated barn behind the ruins of a burned-down house. I made it up the incline to the barn doors okay, but the wheels of Boone's mini-trailer became entrenched, and the spinning rear wheels of his chopper spat mud in an endless spin cycle. Setting my kickstand down, I ran through the downpour to help him lift the trailer free, but the gray mud sucked at the wheels and my boots faced a similar threat. Boone pulled so hard he slipped and fell to his knees.

"Leave it," I said.

"Not without clearing it out!" Fighting his way to his feet, Boone unlatched the trailer doors and passed the M-16s to me. I knew he was right. Then he pulled out the ammo case, which he covered with soup cans, our mess kits, and our Sterno stoves. Using one knee, he slammed the door shut and we staggered to the barn. I threw the latch on the doors and swung one open, releasing the sweet, humid odor of rotting wood. We faced near pitch blackness. Boone set the supplies down just inside the barn and went back for more. I pulled my shake flashlight from my vest pocket, shook it, and aimed its dull flash beam around the barn. Rusted equipment, impossible to identify, cluttered the space: curved blades protruded from the earthen floor like ribs or the reaper's scythe. A ladder led to a loft. My flashlight revealed thick wooden beams, and holes in the roof through which rain fell. No ghouls, though.

I wheeled my bike inside. If we slept, and it stopped raining, and someone came along, they wouldn't get their hands on my pride and joy or the contents of its saddlebags. Boone returned armed with canned food, warm beer, and a kerosene lantern. Kneeling, he laid the supplies on the ground. Through the rain, I would never even know if ghouls lurked nearby.

Boone set the lantern on a hunk of rusted metal three feet off the ground and lit it. I stood at the doors with my M-16.

"Start dinner before I close the doors," I said.

"What am I, your bitch?" The words sounded good natured despite his apparent frustration. I said nothing and he cooked some canned stew over the Sterno stove. I closed the door and latched it from the inside, and we made ourselves as comfortable as we could and ate from our mess kits. The rain falling through the ceiling kept everything damp.

"You think we did the right thing, leaving?" Boone said.

"This is only our second night away from home. Don't tell me you want to go back, because that isn't possible."

"At least we were on familiar ground. And our barn was dry."

"Even if those cops never came back, the property was too large for just the two of us to manage."

"I just feel so cut off. It's weird not knowing what's happening."

"We know what's happening. We just don't know how it's all going down."

"They must outnumber us by now," he said in a slow voice.

"Everyone they kill becomes one of them. Those are bad odds."

"If you can't beat them, eat them."

We slept on the dirt and woke up surrounded by puddles. The rain lasted two days, and we relocated to the loft, where a window with double cedar shutters overlooked Boone's chopper in the driveway. We built a fire below, and because the wood was damp fed worthless U.S. currency into the flames. A trio of ghouls passed the barn, and Boone raised his M-16 to his shoulder.

"What are you doing?"

"Target practice."

"Do you really want to alert every nearby redneck and pig that someone's got this kind of firepower?"

He lowered the weapon. "I'm going to be pissed off if I get killed before I get to use this thing."

He needn't have worried, but he took out his bag of weed anyway and rolled a joint. "Care to join me?"

I shook my head. "I'd rather keep my wits about me."

"Suit yourself." Using a lighter, he fired up. "You may not get many more opportunities."

"That's fine with me."

He sucked in marijuana smoke. "Buzzkill."

I closed my eyes and waited for the rain to stop.

I woke up with sunshine on my face, a nice change of pace. Sitting, I saw Boone using a board from the barn to free the mini-trailer. I waited until he had finished to see if he wanted help, and he gave me the finger.

It felt good to get back on the road, too bad we were running low on gas. We followed signs to the Meshingomesia reservation on the northeastern side of the Mississinewa River, in Liberty Township. Tax-free gasoline and cigarettes, once upon a time. As we neared the reservation's border, we saw eight American Indian men of varying ages standing to greet us with shotguns. We slowed to a stop, Boone a dozen feet behind me, as planned. I made sure to leave my hands on my ape hangers where they could be seen, and hoped Boone did the same.

"How?" a man my age with long hair said, his voice dripping with sarcasm.

I wanted to raise my hands and get off my bike so I could walk closer to them, but I felt more secure with my rifle in reach. "How's it going?"

"What can we do for you fine white men on this happy Tuesday morning?"

Tuesday. I hadn't given any thought to day or date since before the apocalypse.

"We're hoping you'll give us some gas," I said.

The man stared down the barrel of his shotgun. "Why should we give you anything?"

"We could pay you, but I'm guessing money's worthless now."

"Maybe you're worthless now. Maybe you were always worthless. Maybe you were born that way."

I couldn't disagree with him. "We don't want any trouble. If you don't want to help us, we'll just be on our way."

"What makes you think you're in a position to cause trouble? There's eight of us to two of you and our guns are ready."

"I'll give you that. None of you would even break a sweat killing us. But what would the point be?"

"We'd get those bikes and your guns, and whatever you've got in that little trailer. And our ghouls would get some protein."

Turning in my saddle, I saw half a dozen ghouls lumbering in our direction.

"Get down," the Indian said.

He didn't have to tell me twice, and by the time I hit the dirt the armed men fired a volley at the advancing dead things.

"Jesus!" Boone said. I knew he hadn't had enough time to climb out of the chopper, so the Indians fired right over his head.

Rising, I slapped dust off my knees. The Indians relaxed their shotguns—at least they weren't aiming them at us any longer—and I saw the ghouls lying unmoving on the ground.

"You isolated us on these reservations so you wouldn't have to see us," the leader said. "The irony is, you made the reservations self-sufficient. Now our culture is alive and yours is dead. Our society's protected, while yours feeds on itself. We've got gas, power, water. What have you got? The same thing you're leaving here with: nothing. Turn your bikes around and get the hell off Indian land."

It sounded like he had spoken those words before, but I didn't want to say so. I started my engine, turned around, and looked over my shoulder. "Good luck." I don't know why, but I meant it. Maybe they really would keep civilization alive.

"You're going to need it more than we are," the man said.

Boone turned around in a wide circle and I followed him, weaving between the still ghouls so as not to get their ruptured heads all over our wheels.

Just before we hit Logansport, we passed a downed helicopter with a TV station's call letters emblazoned on its side. One rotor blade had shattered on the ground, the body resembled a crushed beer can, and smoke rose from the burning wreckage. We didn't stop to see if there were any survivors.

Cars littered the highway and we saw a procession of pedestrians stumbling towards the city on the horizon. There must have been a hundred of them, resembling the shell-shocked refugees I'd seen on TV news broadcasts before the fall, with tattered clothing and bloodied limbs: men, women, and children. God only knew what had happened to them, but I took it as a good sign that they wanted to reach the same small city we did. Then I heard a deep, ominous wind without experiencing turbulence. I scanned the horizon on either side of Logansport for signs of a tornado, but saw no tunnel forming in the clouds, no hint of green. The sound continued, deepening as we neared the refugees. At the same time that I recognized their lifeless gait, I realized that what I heard was scores of moans layered on top of each other. Smelling their rotting flesh from two hundred yards away I gagged, which caused my bike to wobble on the bloodstained asphalt. I maintained my balance and shot through the crowd, maneuvering around the ghouls when I could and knocking them aside when I couldn't. Since they stared ahead at their destination, they seemed unaware of my approach, so at least I didn't have to battle them.

I wanted to speed up, to get through the daisy chain of reanimated corpses as fast as possible, but my instincts told me to slow down and treat the troop of walking dead like an obstacle course. I had almost cleared the body count when my front wheel slid through a pile of guts that resembled rotting macaroni. An instant of panic seized me as my bike spun out of control, but all I could do was hang on for dear life. Before I knew it, I slid sideways across the pavement, my heart slamming in my chest.

There are only two kinds of bikers in this world: those who have had accidents, and those who are going to have accidents. I've had my share of wipeouts. My ape hangers and my foot rests protected my legs somewhat, and I remained on the road; if I'd flown into a ditch, who knows what damage my bike would have sustained. When it stopped spinning, I found myself staring at Logansport: a few tall buildings surrounded by a lot of smaller ones, with plenty of trees between them. Looking over my shoulder, I saw the advancing horde of ghouls. Worse, they saw me.

The dead things walked in loose rows of five, and ten sunken, unblinking eyes seemed to focus on me at the same time. Their jaws opened and closed as if they wanted to lick their chops, and God help me if they didn't shamble faster. Scrambling out from under my bike, I jerked my rifle free of its holster. As I raised the stock to my shoulder, I saw my left arm had opened up from its elbow to my wrist and my blood flowed freely.

I heard the chopper but saw no sign of Boone. I expected him to race through the ghouls, a passive expression on his face. Instead, he rode up around the left side of the horde, his shades masking his demeanor. That fucker didn't worry about anything. As soon as he cleared my line of fire, I aimed at a ghoul in a Dunkin' Donuts uniform and squeezed the trigger. I missed her head, but a scalp exploded three rows farther back. I'm not exactly the world's greatest marksman under pressure.

My partner pulled over beside me and killed his engine. I aimed at the Dunkin' Donuts ghoul again and took out her right eye. She continued moving, as if she couldn't decide if I'd hit her brain or not, and then toppled on her side and stopped moving. Looking at her made me think of coffee and Boston Cream donuts. Boone opened the trailer door and took out one of the M-16s, which I knew made him feel good. He threw the weapon's safety off, raised it to his shoulder, aimed, and fired—and kept firing. Heads exploded, brains spilled, torsos jerked. Bodies piled on the ground, and soon the ghouls behind them tripped and fell. I like to think I contributed to the pileup, but I admit it was mostly Boone's doing.

"Get going!" he said over the sound of ejecting shells.

I slid my rifle back into holster and picked up my bike, my arm bleeding badly. I got on my saddle, started my engine, and took off, confident that Boone had the situation in hand. It's a good feeling to know someone's got your back when one hundred pus- and maggot-filled ghouls want to turn you into appetizers for the road crew.

I drove ahead half a mile. Along the way, I passed a number of ambitious ghouls who traveled alone, ahead of the pack. I was only too happy to slow down, plant the barrel of my .45 against their temple, and shoot out their head stuffing. If Boone had trouble following the road, he'd have no trouble following the trail of brainless bodies I left behind, not to mention the trail of my blood.

Pulling over to the shoulder, I holstered my weapon and inspected the gash. The wind resistance had blown the blood from the wound up my bicep and over my shoulder, so most of my arm glistened red, and the red stuff kept coming.

Boone pulled alongside me, killed his engine, and pushed his shades into his hair. Looking at my arm, his face turned serious. "You need some darning, hoss."

Opening and closing my fingers, I watched the blood seep out of my wound faster, which was a pretty dumb thing to do. "I reckon so."

Boone hopped out of his saddle and opened the mini-trailer, then returned with two small plastic cases: a First Aid kit and a sewing kit. Watching him bait the sewing needle with thick black thread was more painful than my injury.

"At least give me some warm beer with that," I said.

Boone accomplished his task. "You won't smoke reefer in a barn, but you'll chug a beer on a highway infested with ghouls?"

"I can't think of a better time to get fucked up."

He retrieved a beer for me which I guzzled straight down. Then he sewed up my arm, which disgusted me more than it pained me. He must have pushed that needle through my flesh twenty times, each pull of the thread pulling the seams of my flesh together. As he performed the procedure, I watched the lumbering ghouls draw closer. They struck me as slow and patient, like the tortoise in that story with the hare. At last he severed the thread with his teeth, and tied a little knot. The ghouls got close enough for me to see the whites of their eyes; at least those whose eyelids had rotted away.

"There, you're all fixed up." Boone slapped my back. "Now let's go get some gas."

He dropped into his saddle, started his engine, and took off. Hearing the ghouls' moans, I followed. Someone had to watch his back.

Just slip out the back, Jack, make a new plan, Stan...

Paul Simon

5

Logansport was soaked in blood, and that's no exaggeration. As in Erie, cars were overturned and storefront windows were smashed by looters, with fires burning out of control, but any riots had climaxed and sputtered out like an exhausted lover. Hundreds—possibly thousands—of bodies littered the sidewalks and streets. Blood glistened and baked on the asphalt, and countless ghouls milled about, feasting upon those recently killed or searching for survivors to chew on. We didn't venture into the heart of the city, but instead skirted it, observing the undead population from afar. We pulled over to the sidewalk of a street where several cars had been abandoned and had not been flipped, and took out our hoses. Working with separate vehicles, we each siphoned gas into the tanks of our bikes, then into our spare gas cans. I've always loved the smell of gasoline.

A low moan rose from behind my car, then another and another after that. Looking at each other, we moved between our respective cars. A different sound merged with the moans, accompanying them like a musical instrument: the buzzing of thousands of flies. I saw a dark splotch on the sidewalk, and another, and another—maybe a dozen in all, surrounded by broken glass: pancakes made out of piles of dirty clothing, with blood stains radiating outward like maple syrup. Flies swarmed over them, eating, defecating, laying eggs—an army of black and gold and green. The moans rose from the blood-smeared piles. Moving closer to one of the sticky splotches, I discerned the shapes of broken limbs that almost formed a swastika around a human head, which lay flat on one side, no longer supported by its neck. A single eye focused on me while a shattered jaw worked in a semi-circle, a tongue hanging over shattered teeth. It resembled a broken puppet more than a former human being. Judging by the soggy, wrinkled suit that held the body parts together, the mush had once been a man. He didn't seem to mind the winged insects crawling over his eyeball and on his tongue.

"Good Christ," Boone said.

A few feet away, a woman's face stared out between two mounds of flies I recognized as breasts. I cocked my head to one side, trying to imagine how her body had turned inside out, but the way she kept licking her lips in hunger caused me to look away. A raised knee protruded from the center of another splotch, creating a fleshy, fly infested sun dial. Standing in the cool shadow of a building, I looked up at the sky, which framed twelve floors of steel, concrete, and glass.

"They jumped from the upper floors." Awe dripped from Boone's voice.

"This building isn't burning," I said. "Ghouls drove them out."

"And then these sorry sons of bitches became ghouls after impact."

The pitiful broken creatures twitched and struggled to move. They wanted to devour us, but their bodies lacked the connections necessary for locomotion.

"Should we put them out of their misery?" Boone said.

I shook my head. "It's still a long way to L.A. We can't spare the ammo."

"Promise me that if you ever have to make the same choice about me, you'll find a bullet to spare."

"One way or another, I won't let you suffer like these poor bastards."

The sound of the flies grew maddening. Returning to our bikes, we saw a dozen heaps of rotting flesh shambling towards us at the end of the block, stepping from the sunlit intersection into the shadow of the building above us. Two dozen approached from the other direction.

"Follow the light," I said.

We roared down a five-lane street when Boone tapped his horn and veered left. Decelerating, I made a U-turn and followed him into a driveway that led past a bank, a movie theater, and a McDonalds. I caught up to him beneath those golden arches, which had always looked piss yellow to me. Behind the Mickey D's, a Tops Friendly Market dominated a strip mall. Shopping carts and cars with open doors had been left scattered across the parking lot, and someone had smashed the supermarket's massive windows. I couldn't help but think of my encounter with the ghouls in the frozen foods section at Wegmans, where Deke was bitten.

"I'm not anxious to go grocery shopping again," I said.

"Neither am I." Boone jerked a thumb behind him. "I just want to see a movie."

The theater's old-fashioned marquee bore three titles I'd never heard before.

"You're crazy."

"Those glass doors aren't broken, and most theaters converted to digital projection."

"So what?"

"So, all we need is a generator to supply the juice. The projector works like a Blu Ray player. We can watch all three movies and spend the night here."

"I don't want to watch all three movies. I don't want to watch any of them. I never heard of them."

"I never heard of them either, but I want to watch them. Who knows if I'll ever get the chance again?"

Trees waved in the breeze across the street and deep lawns gave way to what appeared to be a campus. I didn't see ghouls anywhere, but I knew they were out there, and I knew their hunger would bring them to the land of Ronald McDonald and Mayor McCheese.

"I thought you wanted to see America," I said.

"Movies are America."

We drove around to the back of the theater, where a cinderblock wall faced woods separating the plaza from a row of identical, two-story brick buildings. Housing projects, I guessed. Boone used a crowbar to wrest a steel emergency exit door from its frame, but a chain prevented him from opening it all the way. Crouching, he reached inside the darkness.

"That isn't very smart," I said.

Boone grinned. Then his eyes widened and he screamed. I started forward, drawing my .45 from its holster. Boone rose to his feet and the door swung open, revealing the chain in his hand, a simple clip at one end. My partner doubled over with laughter, and then he sank to his knees after I slugged him in the gut. I'm a pretty big guy, and I've got ugly paws from all the fights I've been in. I guess all of my fingers have been broken in one brawl or another, and because bikers don't generally carry Blue Cross Blue Shield, I never went to any emergency rooms, so the broken fingers healed kind of disfigured. That didn't stop me from pulling my pecker or squeezing a trigger, though.

"What did you do that for?" Boone said between gasps when he'd regained his breath.

"Exactly."

I didn't help him to his feet. Instead I opened the door wider and set a cinderblock against it. Inside, dust motes swam in the light. I pulled my Savage 110 from its holster and strode into the theater's rear exit. Boone joined me with his M-16. We both gripped shake flashlights. The dank space reeked of rotten popcorn, and we stood listening to each other's breathing as we faced two metal exit doors which had been painted blue.

"Go on," I said. "You're the one who wants to watch this crap so bad."

Boone pushed the doors open and we faced total darkness, which even swallowed the light behind us. It *felt* dark in there. We aimed our flashlights inside, but the circles of light barely illuminated the movie theater seats, which were not the stadium kind. Locating a small push broom and a pan with a long handle, I propped the exit doors open.

"Let's just wait here a spell."

Our eyes adjusted to the darkness and pretty soon I saw the outline of the seats, maybe twenty rows' worth, with two aisles dividing them into three sections. There may have been 350 seats in total. I don't think I've ever stood anywhere as quiet as that empty movie theater.

"I don't want to leave the bikes outside," I said.

"There's nobody out there to take them," Boone said.

"We'll see. Other than those cops, we haven't dealt with any scavengers yet, but I guarantee they're out there. It will be a good day for anyone who takes our gear."

We went outside and wheeled our bikes into the fire exit, where we turned them around so they faced the outside doors in case we had to beat a hasty retreat. A distant droning grew louder and I thought about the flies. At first it sounded like a lawn mower, then more like a motorcycle... but higher. After exchanging wide-eyed looks, we ran back outside and searched the sky.

"There!" Boone said.

In a cloudy section of the sky a small propeller plane wobbled from side to side, its wings telegraphing its inevitable fall from grace. It had been weeks since I'd seen any airborne aircraft. The plane dipped low, then streaked overhead, its engine whining as it cut a swath through the sky. Following its flight path, I estimated its destination: an eight-story building half a mile away.

"Oh, fuck," Boone said.

Sure enough, the plane leveled off but continued its descent toward the building. The pilot could have avoided the collision if he'd so desired, but instead he flew his plane straight into the building. Except for its tail, the plane vanished inside the building at about the sixth floor, dust and rubble spilling over the edge and falling to the street below, which was obscured by trees. I half expected to see a fireball, but nothing exploded. The plane must have been flying on close to an empty fuel tank.

"God damn," Boone said. "Why the hell did he do that?"

"Maybe he ran out of fuel."

"He could have landed on any street here!"

"Then maybe he saw enough from up there."

It was a sobering thought, and we returned to the theater, where we had to wait for our eyes to adjust to the darkness all over. We moved up the closest aisle, our boots thudding on carpets as hard as cement thanks to years' worth of soda spills. Our flashlight beams moved over the seats and between the rows, and humid darkness pressed around us. Ghouls could have been hiding anywhere in there and we wouldn't have known it. My dim circle of artificial moonlight moved over the fabric on the walls, revealing large speakers. Portals from the upstairs projection booth overlooked the auditorium. A pair of doors admitted us to a small lobby with bathrooms and a water fountain on our left, two gray metal doors on our right, and a domed ceiling. I counted six doors ahead of us and pushed one open. Sunlight flooded a second lobby through six glass doors facing the driveway outside. I squinted at poster cases lining the wall on our right and a door that led into a box office next to the doors. On the left, a concession stand which had been stripped bare taunted us.

Boone flipped a countertop door and walked behind the stand as if he worked there. He used the butt of his M-16 to smash the locks on the back cabinets. Within seconds Starburst, Skittles, M&Ms, and Jujubes covered the glass top of the empty display case. The candy boxes flowed over the edge and fell on the floor like it was Halloween.

"You're going to make a pretty pathetic ghoul when all of your teeth fall out," I said.

"I don't watch the movies without candy."

"You're living in a world of make believe."

"I will be soon enough." Boone stuffed his pockets, then opened all the doors separating the lobbies, and all the auditorium doors, allowing light to seep into the darkness.

"You do that like a professional monkey."

"Back home, I worked at the North Park when I was a kid. That was best the best job I ever had. Me and the cashier used to resell used ticket stubs and pocket the cash, and make out in the back row. I did her right behind the screen once, while a movie was playing. The screen was all lit up, and we were naked, and we could see all the people through the transparent screen, staring right at us, but they couldn't see us. It was awesome."

Boone opened one gray metal door and discovered cleaning supplies, then the other, which opened onto a stairway. Without waiting for me, he started upstairs. I followed him up the narrow stairway, which had cinderblock walls. Dull yellow light illuminated the way ahead, and we emerged into a long booth with three monster projectors facing the portals. Sunlight caused the dirty yellow blinds to glow. Boone raised them and light filtered through filthy windows overlooking a flat roof outside. He moved to one of the projectors and studied it with the aid of his flashlight.

"Just like I thought. No one projects film anymore, except museums."

"Even they don't do it now..."

Boone walked over to some breaker boxes, popped their metal doors open, and flipped switches with no results. I felt sorry for him.

"Did you really think there was any juice?"

Ignoring me, he walked to the back of the booth and into a room. Moments later, he stepped out and moved through another door. "Come here!"

I joined him in a storage room crowded floor to ceiling with discarded machinery.

"There!" With a triumphant grin he pointed to the middle of the junk heap.

"'There,' what?"

"That's a generator in a projection booth. We have gas. Magic!"

I laughed. "What a piece of junk! There's no way it still runs."

He sneered. "We'll make it run. We fix our bikes all the time. Look around you: we have all the tools and parts we need."

"How long do you plan for us to stay here?"

Passing me, he slapped my arm. "As long as it takes."

I admit it was hard not to get caught up in his enthusiasm. The hardest part was pulling the generator out of the junk pile: we had to start from the top and work our way down, stacking dusty equipment in the main booth as we jammed multicolored candy into our mouths for energy. We took the Generac apart, cleaned it, oiled it, and replaced a belt. Downstairs, we retrieved our gas can from the mini-trailer. It wasn't as scary walking through the theater with sunlight on our side, but the light faded when we returned to the stairway. Upstairs, we opened a window, positioned the generator on the roof, ran a cable inside to the circuit breakers, and emptied our gas can.

"This had better be a good movie," I said.

"It will probably be the last one we ever see, which will make it great."

The moment of truth arrived: wind blew our hair in our faces, and from that height we saw pretty far down the street: an empty bus with a blood-streaked windshield and broken windows lay on its side; the back half of a pickup truck protruded from the front of a Wendy's; a police car had been overturned; and dozens of skeletons wearing tattered clothing lay on the street, sidewalks, and lawns—their bones picked clean. Boone pushed a primer bulb, closed the choke, and flipped a switch. The generator coughed and sputtered to noisy life, spewing bluish smoke. As Boone climbed inside, a parade of dead citizens marched up Main Street to investigate the ruckus. Standing at the roof's edge, I studied the ghouls: black, white, Hispanic, male, female, adult, child. A man in a greasy mechanic's jumpsuit lumbered shoulder to shoulder with a skinny boy with a green Mohawk that had collapsed; a heavyset woman in a hospital gown walked with her mouth open; a security guard walked in step with a black girl who wore a hoodie. People from all walks of life, brought together in death. And they looked hungry.

Over the generator's roar I heard music coming from inside. I climbed back into the booth, where several LED lights glowing on a stack of metal boxes which reminded me of Promo the Robot, the sidekick on the old *Rocket Ship 7* show. An obnoxious commercial came over the speaker in the cabinet.

"That's the THX sound system." Boone stood between a projector and a metal cabinet. "The projector has juice, the Blu Ray player's on, and the Tivoli lights are on in the aisles downstairs. I can't get the house lights up, though. We'll know what's up with the sound when we get down there." He picked up a remote control and pressed a button, which triggered a beam of light that cut through the darkness like a laser beam as music blasted in the auditorium. Leaning close to a portal, I saw the wide rectangular screen filled with light and color. A movie trailer!

Boone and I traded excited looks and ran downstairs with our guns. In the lobby, I froze in my tracks: two dozen ghouls stood outside the glass doors, staring in at us with hungry eyes. Ignoring them, Boone ran into the auditorium. I walked closer to the front doors. Every eye stared at me and dead palms and fingertips pawed at the glass, leaving an oily residue. A dead little girl knocked on the glass. It's weird to stand before creatures that want to tear your flesh open and eat your organs. Using the toes of my boots, I kicked up the stops on each of the doors separating the lobbies. The doors swung shut, cutting off the light and the hungry stares. In the auditorium, the images on the screen illuminated the seats and I saw Boone positioning himself in the middle. I walked into the same row and sat about six seats away from him.

Three more trailers played for Hollywood blockbusters that would never open: *Alpha Flight; Terminator Revenge;* and *Star Wars Episode VII: A New Sith.* Boone cheered at each title. Animated spotlights highlighted the 20th Century Fox logo, and I wondered how many times I had seen it in my life, and if I would ever see it again. I doubted I would; these days I treated every experience like a swan song. The feature started: *Death Machine,* a vigilante action film starring Bruce Willis, a one-time TV actor who had become a big movie star, and Gary Dugan, another TV actor who had been poised for success when everything fell apart. In the flick, Dugan plays a guy who takes a job as an undercover armed guard while waiting to be called to the NYPD police academy. He works for a security outfit that picks up money from movie theaters at the end of the night and deposits it in night drop boxes at banks. Willis plays a retired cop working for the same outfit, who takes Dugan under his wing. On Dugan's first night on the job, he and Willis are robbed while leaving a Times Square theater, and Willis takes a paralyzing bullet to his spine. Waiting in the hospital to hear how Willis is doing, Dugan learns from his wife that he's been accepted into the police academy. Willis, driven by a desire for revenge, teaches himself to walk again while Dugan trains to become a cop. Willis becomes a vigilante, Dugan a cop, and the two men are pitted on a collision course.

I liked the first half of the film. It was more realistic than I expected, without the ridiculous CGI special effects that ruin so many movies. The acting was pretty good, too: Willis is more interesting as an old bald guy than he was as a young guy with a toupee. Dugan was okay. There was a great car chase and two good shootouts before I sensed we weren't alone in the darkened theater. Sitting up, I looked around. To my left, three figures sat behind us; to my right, six more. Eight more ghouls sat behind us, which made at least seventeen in all. I'd never seen a ghoul sit before; I didn't know it was possible. They always shambled this way or that way, but these men, women, and teenagers sat glued to their seats, staring at the screen. Were they watching the movie, or were they merely transfixed by the light? The light from the screen flickered on their rotten features and highlighted their drawn-in cheeks and sunken eyes. I'll say this much for the dead: at least they didn't talk during the movie, and there wasn't a cell phone in sight.

Seeing my rigid posture, Boone sprang up in his seat, his boots slapping the concrete floor as his head jerked from side to side. On either side of us, ghouls stumbled down the aisles, fumbling in the darkness for places to plant their bloated asses. My partner gripped his M-16 in both hands, readying to fire. Creeping forward—so as not to block the screen from the ghouls sitting behind us?—I grabbed one of his elbows and shook my head.

"Look at them."

I felt his body relax as he took in the sight of a good thirty ghouls watching Bruce Willis and Gary Dugan shoot up Times Square.

"Holy shitfuck…"

I waited for the ghouls to clamber out of their seats and lurch toward us, but they remained seated, their full attention on the movie.

"What should we do?" Boone said.

"I'm all for getting the hell out of here—slowly."

Boone cast a longing glance at the screen, then at the ghouls.

"Don't even think about it."

More ghouls filed into the theater. Some of them lingered in the aisle, too captivated by the onscreen mayhem to look for a seat. Stooping, we duck walked to the end of the aisle. My grip on my Savage 110 tightened as I stepped around a ghoul who stood with his back to me. I kept expecting the damned thing to reach out and grab my shoulder, and it infuriated me that I couldn't hear Boone's footsteps behind me over the artificial gunfire issuing from the speakers. At the exit doors I finally turned to see if Boone was behind me, and he pushed me through the doors and into the dark exit. For a moment the flickering light from the projector highlighted the curves of our bikes; then the doors closed, trapping us in pitch darkness. I took out my flashlight, shook it to life, and heard the doors swing open behind Boone.

"Shit!" Boone threw himself against the doors and angled his body at a forty five degree angle to keep them shut. Fists pounded on the other side of the door. "Find something to wedge behind these handles!"

I searched the darkness with my flashlight. A broom looked too flimsy to hold the ghouls at bay. So did a dustpan with a long handle. In a closet space with no door I found a long metal pole used for changing light bulbs.

"Hurry up!"

Seizing the pole, I ran back to Boone, popping the end of the flashlight into my mouth, and slid the pole between the handles. Rotating a metal ring near one end of the pole, I pulled out an extension. Then I closed the ring and wedged the pole between two walls. "That should hold them long enough."

With his back pressed against the doors, Boone aimed his M-16 at the remaining exit door. "Let's see what we've got out there."

I pushed the panic bar on the door and threw it open. Dusk had settled over the parking lot out back but orange and pink light streaked the sky. Stepping outside and seeing no ghouls, I propped the cinderblock against the door again.

More fists pounded on the doors behind Boone, which opened just an inch before he forced them closed again. Taking out my keys, I hopped onto my hog, slid my rifle into its holster, and started my engine. The roar grew deafening inside the exit, and gas fumes filled my lungs. I launched myself through the doorway like a rocket, then planted one boot on the ground and turned in a half circle. I jerked my rifle free again and aimed it in Boone's general direction, which must have made him feel great. He leapt into the saddle of his chopper, lay his M-16 across his lap, and started his engine. The doors burst open behind him, then ricocheted against the pole and closed again. They opened with greater force, but the pole held steady. Boone had to exit slowly, so the mini-trailer didn't tip over. The doors opened with greater force, bending the pole, and I held my rifle steady. As soon as he saw that the mini-trailer had navigated the single step to the ground, Boone raced away from the theater. A trio of silhouetted ghouls staggered through the exit doors. Holstering my rifle, I peeled out after Boone.

As we circled the lot, I saw what appeared to be a hundred ghouls on Main Street, only they weren't moving: they stood in line, waiting to enter the theater. We never figured out how they found a way inside—maybe through one of the adjoining buildings—but we knew this: *Death Machine,* starring Bruce Willis and Gary Dugan, was *The Last Picture Show* of its day.

Carry on my wayward son...
There'll be peace when you are done...

Kansas

4

Kansas is cold in October, and we took to wearing our leather motorcycle jackets over sweatshirts. We also collected a couple of helmets along the way. Who wants to catch an ear infection during a worldwide ghoul epidemic?

Avoiding the cities, we passed empty fields, isolated churches, and spinning windmills. We were smack dab in the middle of the country, but less than halfway to L.A. from where we'd started, our progress slowed because we stopped to siphon gas whenever the opportunity arose, not just when we needed it. Our canned food held up, but our canned beer ran out, and Boone complained he was running low on weed.

We must have been three quarters of the way across the state when we saw them: hundreds of wooden crosses on either side of the highway, each one protruding twenty feet from the earth—and each one occupied. The crucified ghouls fixed their stares on us rather than at the heavens above. Their fingers twitched, their tongues rolled, and their heads turned from side to side. A ghoul with restricted movement pretty much looks like a regular corpse until a spasm of dead flesh catches your attention.

"Someone's been busy," Boone said. We had slowed to a stop where the crosses started.

"There's gotta be two hundred of them."

"Yeah, and none of them are white."

Now masked by dead gray flesh, the ghouls had all been minorities at one time: black, Hispanic, Asian, Arabic.

"The KKK took my baby away."

My stomach turned queasy. Why would anyone possibly separate ghouls into non-white and white camps? And where were the white ghouls? Had they received proper burials? A frightening thought occurred to me: what if these minorities had been crucified when they were still alive? "Let's get out of here."

"Yeah."

Then we heard the sirens of cherry tops speeding toward us from both directions on the highway. We had discussed what we would do if any of the militant cops we'd heard about ever cornered us, and had decided to go out in a blaze of glory. Unfortunately, we hadn't planned on half a dozen police cars and another half dozen redneck pickups bearing down on us before we had much of a chance to react. Boone gave me a wild-eyed look and I shook my head.

The lead cherry tops circled us, kicking up dust which rose to the tortured-looking ghouls who had died and risen for our sins. The cars in the middle of the two caravans circled the first cars, which had braked, and the trucks circled the outer perimeter. You'd think we were Osama bin Laden.

The first cops appeared behind their vehicles, Glocks and pump action shotguns drawn and Kevlar vests strapped taut. I waited for someone to shout "Freeze!" or "Police!" When no one did, I raised my hands all on my own, and Boone followed my lead. When the last vehicle had stopped moving, a man in a sheriff's uniform, with a metal star pinned to the front of his cowboy hat, strode toward us. He wore mirrored sunglasses and a sour puss.

I can't say I hate all cops—just the ones I've met. I've got no objection to the idea of cops, but it's always seemed to me that the worst Neanderthals are drawn to that club, the guys who played football in high school, tormented outcasts, and banged cheerleaders on prom night. In Nazi Germany, they carted away the Jews; down south during the civil rights movement, they unleashed attack dogs on blacks; on college campuses across the country, they beat students protesting the war. It's a power thing. I know I'm generalizing, but I believe you have to fear people who can take away your rights, and as I watched this asshole march towards us I remembered every asshole pig I ever saw in a movie, from *Cool Hand Luke* to *Live and Let Die*.

At least twenty men and women pointed guns at us as the sheriff looked us up and down and checked out our plates.

"You boys are a ways from home," he said. "What brings you to Kansas?"

"We're just passing through," Boone said. "We're heading to Hollywood."

The sheriff grinned. "You're crazy."

Some of the hardened faces around us laughed without smiling.

The sheriff pointed at my rifle. "It's not exactly legal to ride around like that." He moved his finger to Boone's M-16. "And that sure as hell isn't. Where did you get it?"

My muscles tensed.

"My brother collected guns," Boone said. "He died back in Buffalo. I kept this as a keepsake."

"Men have to protect themselves," I said.

Sheriff Asshole stepped back. "Call us old fashioned, but here in Kansas, we've still got laws. We're going to have to take you in."

I glared at him.

"You can come peacefully, you can come dead, or you can come undead. My choice."

With our hands still raised, we got off our bikes. Half a dozen deputies with brush cuts, hard jaws, and round biceps encircled us. As they cuffed our hands behind our backs I stared at the emaciated ghouls who wanted to eat me. The cops shoved us into the backs of separate cherry tops, loaded our bikes into the pickups, and drove us along a number of side roads. We passed abandoned houses, empty barns, and the occasional ghoul before arriving at the Sheriff's department, a two-story orange brick building with a flat roof. The front lawn had been mowed and the American flag waved on a pole. Everything appeared as normal as maple syrup except for the chain-link fence surrounding the property. An electric gate swung open, admitting us to the parking lot, which was filled with civilian vehicles as well as cherry tops.

When the deputies hauled me out of their car, I was relieved to see Boone. They marched us to the building, up granite steps, and inside, where few deputies and civilian staff members gave us curious looks. They had electricity, and things appeared to be business as usual. One deputy had me empty my pockets and identify my belongings as he inventoried them. Then he fingerprinted me and showed me to a cell. At least it was clean. They brought Boone in and put him in the next cell. As we sat there waiting, other deputies brought in our guns and laid them on a table near the counter. It was quite an impressive arsenal, I had to admit.

A woman in her late twenties walked over to the cells. She wore her dark hair pulled back into a ponytail, and she wore a navy blue dress that ended above her knees. "What would you guys like for dinner? We have roast beef and turkey. The side dishes are the same."

Although she spoke in a level voice, I detected desperation in her voice, and there was something in her eyes that I couldn't quite make out.

"Roast beef," I said.

"Turkey," Boone said.

The meal was better than fine: fresh and cooked to perfection, better than we'd eaten in a long time. When we'd finished, the deputies took us into separate rooms and interviewed us. My steroid case asked very general questions; I kept waiting for him to get to the good stuff, but he never did. They took us back to our cells, where we sat and stared at a wall mounted TV that would never air programming again. I took off my boots and lay down on my cot, which wasn't half uncomfortable.

"Hey, can I get some coffee?" Boone said.

"We just have tea," a deputy said.

"How about some pop?"

"Kool-Aid."

Boone sighed, and the springs of his cot squeaked. My brain relaxed, but I hadn't quite fallen asleep when a door opened and closed, followed by footsteps.

"Good evening, Mrs. Mayor."

"Hi, George. How are your adorable munchkins?" a woman said. Her loud voice grated on me right away.

"Growing faster than me and the wife can outfit them," the deputy said.

Curious to see this female mayor, I sat up on my cot and just about fell off it. The woman standing beside the sheriff wore black buccaneer boots, white knickers, a gold vest, and a frilly blouse beneath an ornate overcoat straight out of the American Revolution. She also wore horn rimmed glasses and a Colonial Tricorn hat trimmed in gold. If not for her feminine figure and attractive features, she could have been George Washington. She came over to our cells, followed by the sheriff. Her eyes may have been beautiful, but they were a little too shiny for sanity and bordered on being crossed.

"Well, hi, there!" she said, her pink lipstick glistening.

"Hi," I said.

"I'm Mayor Bachlin. What's your name?"

"Walker."

"Just one name, like that Madonna whore?"

"I suppose so."

She turned her head. "How about you?"

"Boone."

"Welcome to Heartland, outside Topeka."

"That's a pretty name," Boone said, turning on the charm.

"Thank you, I came up with it myself. One of my advisors suggested New Washington. I said, 'No, thank you. Everything that's wrong with this country comes from Washington, D.C. Things just haven't been the same since they put that monkey in the White House. We need a name that reflects who we really are.'"

I gestured at the bars. "I don't exactly feel like a guest."

"Oh, don't be so dramatic. We're just keeping you here while we figure out what to do with you."

I didn't like the sound of that. "You could just let us be on our way."

"Nope, can't do that. There's a fifty dollar room charge for the cell, and another fifteen for the dinner you ate. Plus your vehicles are impounded. That's seventy five dollars a day. Right now, you each owe us one hundred and forty dollars, and we only take gold. Do you have any gold?"

"No."

"Then you'll have to work it off. Only, tomorrow night you'll owe another $140, plus another $25 for breakfast and lunch. At least you don't have to pay taxes on that. No more taxes, hallelujah, Lord be praised!"

"Work it off how?" Boone said.

"Can either of you boys write?"

I was glad Boone didn't throw me under the bus.

"No? Too bad, we've got a lot of textbooks that need rewriting. There's so much work to do if we're going to get things right this time, but by golly, the FFO—that's the Founding Fathers' Order—is going to put America the way the good Lord intended. It's as plain as day that you're both white, you've got that in your favor. You're not faggots, are you?"

"No, ma'am," Boone said. "We're as straight as lumber."

"Glad to hear it." The mayor winked at me. "Sheriff Acorn will make sure you're treated well. Sheriff, move these men to a dormitory first thing in the morning, before you assign them to their work details, okay?"

"Yes, Madame Mayor."

"And let them spend the night in the same cell since they aren't queer. Give them a deck of cards so they can entertain themselves."

"Yes, ma'am."

The mayor turned and left, followed by her uniformed shadow. Two of the deputies moved Boone into my cell. We played cards for an hour and then went to bed. We didn't speak. We didn't have to. We both knew that we had to get the hell out of Dodge.

The next morning, we ate a full breakfast, which was a nice change of pace. Then four deputies loaded us into a prison truck and drove us along a dirt road to a farm surrounded by a chain-link fence. When we got off the bus, they pressed our guns into our hands.

"Second amendment," a deputy said.

I felt better already. They took us into a barn which had been converted into a shelter of sorts: scores of cots covered the floor. I preferred my cell.

"People who are assigned to work details but can't pay their way stay here," the deputy said. "Everybody works for everything he consumes; there are no more free rides. If you don't pull your own weight, we'll use you for target practice. Then we'll let you rise and we'll use you for target practice again. Understand?"

"We get the picture."

"Find yourselves a couple of bunks while I go find Rochester, the overseer."

"Overseer?" Boone said as the deputy walked away.

We found two cots that appeared to be free and sat on them. A woman with long, straight hair hurried inside and came over to us. It took a moment for me to recognize her as the civilian who had served us our dinner at the sheriff's station.

"I'm Marion. I live in the woman's dormitory. Listen carefully: do whatever they tell you to do, or they'll kill you. The only way to stay alive is to pretend to be like them."

She ran out of the barn as quickly as she had entered it. Boone just stared at me.

A few minutes later, the deputy returned with a tall man with a receding hairline.

"This is Rochester. He owns this farm. He'll put you boys to work. Do whatever he tells you, and you'll get along just fine. Good luck." The deputy left.

Rochester admired Boone's M-16. "You boys came with some nice accessories. You know how to shoot those things?"

"We manage," I said.

"Good, glad to hear it. You'll spend the day with me today, so I can teach you the rules. Tomorrow I'll assign you to your regular details, but for now, we're hunting ghouls."

We climbed into the back of Rochester's truck and he drove us off the farm. The truck passed a gated community that looked like something out of a TV show: scores of identical houses with manicured lawns and children playing, the community surrounded by a high brick wall. Rochester took us through some woods and parked on the side of the road, near a field. We joined him in front of the truck, where he jerked his thumb in the direction we'd just come.

"That community back there is where all the job creators live, including the mayor. They've kept things running: the juice, the water, the gas pumps. Our job is to protect them and make things easier for them, so they can keep providing for us. Someone's got to run the show, and someone's got to do the labor. It's the natural way."

I never thought of myself as a mule, but I kept that thought to myself because of Marion's warning. Instead I showed Rochester my wounded arm, which had grown purple around Boone's sutures.

"Since civilization's thriving here, you think I can see a doctor? I did this on the road and my partner sewed me up. It's sore as hell."

Rochester studied my arm, and I knew he was looking for bite marks. "Oh, we've got doctors, but they don't work for free. Why should they? Earn yourself some gold, and when you've got enough, make an appointment. They barter too, but I didn't see you boys with no chickens. I reckon your arm won't fall off before you earn a week's wages."

"I reckon so." I didn't want to seem disagreeable.

Rochester walked us through the woods. "Topeka's about ten miles from here, so the fields and woods are lousy with ghouls. We send posses out every day, but more of these things just keep coming. Ghoul patrol is good work for the right kind of man. Looking at the two of you, I have to figure you're the right kind of men."

We didn't argue. He took led us to the crest of a hill, where we looked down at three dozen ghouls roaming a field like cattle, only there were no people down there for them to graze on. The undead men, women and children had brown, black and yellow skin.

Rochester spat. "A lot of them come from the projects, near as I can figure. The cities are lost and the suburbs are failing. Everyone's moving to the country for a better life, even the dead."

He raised the stock of his Winchester to his shoulder, sighted on a black female ghoul, and blew her brain out the back of her head. The other ghouls turned in semi-circles, reacting to the sound of the gunshot rolling over the sparse treetops, but paid no attention to their fallen comrade.

"They're dumber than animals," Rochester said. "Let's go get the rest of them."

And so we wandered down into the field, where we massacred the ghouls. But can you massacre beings who are already dead? I told myself, *That isn't a woman lumbering toward me, it's already a corpse. That isn't a little boy, about the same age my son was the last time I saw him; it's a ghoul. That isn't someone's grandfather; it's just a reanimated mishmash of flesh and bone.* But their eyes said otherwise. We might just as well have been executing homeless people.

It wasn't just a massacre; some of them fled into the woods, and we had to split up and chase them down. I never took to hunting deer, and I sure as hell didn't enjoy hunting people, even if they were already dead. It was hard, emotionally draining work that only got worse when we regrouped back in the field, surrounded by motionless corpses. From his backpack, Rochester removed three big hooks and handed one to me and the other to Boone.

"You know what these are for. We want to create one big pile, not three or four little ones, and that means dragging those ones out in the woods back here. After that, we'll break for lunch. Trust me, you don't want to eat while the bodies are burning. There's no worst stink on earth."

As I walked back into the woods with my rifle slung over my shoulder and my big hook in my hand, I couldn't even think about eating.

"Hey, Johnny, what are you rebelling against?"
"Whadda you got?"

Peggy Maley and Marlon Brando in *The Wild One*

3

We returned to our dorm at dusk. Dozens of men occupied the barn when we entered it. I pulled off my boots and lay on my cot.

"You stink like death," a man next to me said.

I looked at him: skinny, short, and weasel faced. I must have reeked for him to speak to a big guy like me like that. I was about to tell him to fuck off when he stood up and pointed out the barn doors.

"We've got a bunch of troughs set up for laundry. You might want to get to it before you fall asleep, so your clothes have time dry. There are showers in the bathrooms."

I glanced at Boone, who nodded, and we walked outside and washed our clothes, then hung them on a clothesline to dry in the cold air. We each had only two or three changes of clothes. The bathrooms were located in a separate building: four for the men and presumably the same number for women. The hot water felt good; so did the soap. Afterward, we went to the cafeteria, which appeared to have been a triple garage at one time. We served ourselves rice and beef stew, then sat at a picnic table. Before we could eat, one of Rochester's goons came in.

"Before y'all dig in, ya gotta say grace."

I was about to bow my head and pretend to pray when I saw everyone else get on their feet. Placing one hand over his chest, Rochester recited the

Christian version of the Pledge of Allegiance. I put my hand over my heart and joined in. It felt like someone was scrubbing my brain. After grace we sat down, and within seconds, Marion joined us. She had showered too; her hair gleamed like that of a model in a shampoo commercial.

"How was your day?" she said. "I bet you're both exhausted."

Neither one of us answered. It's better not to talk about some things, especially at the table.

"Here's the thing: I work in the police station, and I've got access to the keys to your bikes."

I raised my eyebrows. Something told me Marion wasn't about to risk her life for two strangers.

"Take me with you, and I'll get you out of here."

Boone sipped his stew. "I'm not saying we're interested in your proposition, and I'm not saying we're not. How do we know we can trust you? You could just be setting us up."

"You've been here long enough to see that things aren't right. The first thing the mayor did was illegalize abortion. According to her, every woman in the compound needs to become a baby machine and replenish the living population. Can you believe that shit? They're rewriting the textbooks to eliminate all references to evolution; Creationism is in. Science? Forget about it. Social programs? Gone with the wind, baby. We've got the haves and the have-nots, forget about a middle class. How about ethnic cleansing? Have you noticed how lily-white the people here are, except for those poor crucified bastards at the edge of town?"

Marion didn't seem to care that neither one of us answered her questions.

"Mayor Bachlin was a former PTA president before she got elected to office. For a year she did nothing but go after municipal employees and replace them with her own family members. You can bet none of her enemies live in that fancy gated community. Her husband used to own a hardware store; now he's in charge of budget. He's the one behind this whole gold scheme! We've got our own currency here, for Christ's sake. People say Bachlin's screwing Sheriff Acorn. It's because of him that everyone fell into line. The mayor, her husband, and the sheriff have kept things together so far, and people are going along with this Founding Fathers' Order of theirs. They closed down the schools, and they expect all of the baby machines to stay home and home school their kids. These nuts have been waiting for some catastrophe like this to happen."

"Get to the part about helping us get out of here," I said.

"I work the night shift. The bus takes me to the sheriff's department in half an hour. You boys have to get out of here and find your way there after midnight, when those fascist pigs change shifts. But you can't just drive up to the building—they'll see you from half a mile away. Get close, then abandon whatever vehicle you bring and walk the rest of the way. Go around to the back, that's where they keep all the impounded vehicles, and there's a lot of them. Most of the people on this farm are outsiders who wandered too close to town. I take my break at 1:00 a.m. That's the best time for me to pop out there and see if you're around. Whatever you do, don't make any noise."

She stood and hurried out of the canteen.

We were so tired that we fell asleep, surrounded by all the other workers, around 8:00 p.m.. Before I drifted off, I heard rifle shots. Someone must have been picking off ghouls at the fence. I woke up to laughter in the barn a couple of times: some of our companions were making the best of their situation. Then I woke up to the sound of dogs barking around twelve. Sitting up, I saw no movement around me. I shook Boone's shoulder and he sat up without saying a word, and we gathered our guns and our boots and we tiptoed outside. Beyond the farmhouse where Rochester lived with his family I saw two armed men standing at the fence with their backs to us. A dozen ghouls stood moaning on the other side of the fence, which is why the dogs were barking. I figured Rochester had left orders for no shooting late at night so he could get some sleep, and it was easy to imagine what the morning wake-up call sounded like.

We pulled on our boots and crossed the grass, stopping only to lay our weapons on the ground behind Rochester's pickup. The guards didn't hear us over the barking dogs until it was too late. We put them in choke holds, and they dropped their weapons without firing them to claw at our arms. I didn't feel my guy's fingernails through the leather sleeve of my MC jacket. Neither man was able to scream, and they thrashed around like beached fish, but we didn't let go. I guess we could have choked them out and left them alive, but they would have awakened a minute or so later, and we would have been in deep trouble. So we finished the job right, and they slipped into the night without making a sound. I didn't release mine until I knew he was finished, and I smelled his shit soon after, when I was searching his pockets. I'm no choir boy.

The dogs barked louder, and I found a set of keys.

Boone ran back to the truck, where he loaded our guns into the back before popping the driver's side door open. He switched off the dome light and disappeared beneath the dashboard to hotwire the engine. I inserted the keys on the ring into the padlocks on the gate and slipped the locks off one by one and dropped them on the ground. Facing the truck, I saw Boone behind the wheel. He waved one arm out the window, so I ran over to him, pulled an M-16 out of the back, and climbed into the passenger side. Holding two ignition wires together, he worked his magic and the engine chugged to life. He switched on the headlights, illuminating the gate ahead and the faces of the ghouls peering in at us, and floored the gas. We rocketed forward, smashed through the gate, and cleared the property. Boone twisted the steering wheel and turned onto the main road, so that I faced the work farm. Then he backed up while I lowered the window, so we were perpendicular to the ghouls lurching through the gateway. I fired a short burst into the air, then aimed the gun and took out three of the ghouls. A light brightened in the farmhouse, and armed figures emerged from the barn. At least the workers stood a fighting chance.

We knew the general way back to the sheriff's department, but it was hard to guess where we should dump the truck. Hearing sirens ahead, Boone pulled behind some trees on the side of the road and three cherry tops sped by, no doubt heading to the farm. So far, so good: at least we knew we were headed in the right direction. When we saw the lights ahead, Boone killed our headlights and slowed the truck to a crawl. He turned left into a field a quarter mile away from the sheriff's department. Getting out, we armed ourselves.

"It's dark," Boone said. "If those things are out there, we'll never see them until it's too late."

"We'll walk side by side. Take your time, keep your gun ready."

"Maybe we should jog."

"No way: if either one of us twists an ankle, we're in deep shit."

Boone spat. "Deeper than we already are? Jesus, if society's going to crumble, I wish it would get on with it already."

We started forward. Crickets chirped, frogs croaked, and stars twinkled. No dead things attacked us. Reaching the fenced-in rear of the sheriff's department, we saw several mounds of burned bodies. Parking lot lights illuminated at least fifty impounded vehicles, and my heartbeat quickened when I saw my hog. We stood at the gate, and Marion appeared from the darkness, wearing a green army flak jacket with patches sewed on. I laughed when I saw the peace sign. Using a ring of keys, she unlocked the padlock on the gate and pulled a chain free. I flipped up the latch and swung the gate open, and she dropped the chain and flung the keys into one of the piles of bodies.

"Half the night force just took off," she said. "Are you guys responsible for that?"

I nodded. "There's some ghoul trouble on Old MacDonald's farm."

"That makes it easier to get out of here, but harder to get out of town. Those good old boys will be looking for us."

She held out one set of ignition keys in each hand, and we took what belonged to us. Then she gestured to her backpack. "I've got your spare ammo, but you can kiss that canned food goodbye."

"What about my weed?" Boone said.

"Sorry."

He actually looked at the back of the department, as if he considered going inside to claim what belonged to him. "Son of a bitch, I bet they smoked it, too."

"I filled up your gas tanks and stashed two gas cans in your trailer. Let's get the fuck out of here."

I climbed onto my bike and Marion climbed on behind me and linked her arms around my sternum. She was a good-looking woman with a nice body, so I didn't mind. When Boone looked settled in his saddle, I started my hog and took off. I led the way through the field on the other side of the compound, so we emerged onto the road on the other side of the station, and we sped away. We didn't pass the crucified ghouls, so at least we weren't backtracking.

I didn't like driving at night. Occasionally, we'd come upon a ghoul, wandering aimlessly on the pavement, his features ghostly in the glare of our headlights; we'd drive around it and keep going. After a steady hour of riding, I pulled over and Boone did the same. The three of us got off our bikes and stood in the middle of the road. We saw no cherry tops.

"Would they let us go, just like that?" I said.

"Acorn's men may like posses, but I can't see Bachlin authorizing that gas expenditure. The farther away we get, the safer we are."

We got back on our bikes and rode until dawn. This time when we pulled over, Marion opened her backpack and passed out sandwiches and little bags of potato chips.

"That's all there is, so make it last. We need to go shopping. Where are we heading?"

I wasn't sure how I felt about her use of "we." She had gotten us our bikes back, so I supposed we had to take her with us.

"Hollywood," I said.

She snorted. "Hollywood's going to be as bad as any other city. They're all overrun with ghouls. Do you want to end up as a combo meal?"

"It's a place," Boone said.

"It's a death trap. We should go to Canada. There are fewer people there, so less trouble."

It bothered me that we thought alike.

"I want to see America," Boone said.

Marion laughed and Boone turned red.

"What's there to see? America is dead. It died even before the ghouls rose. It was nothing but a bunch of corporate dictators, brainwashed buffoons, and gun-loving male chauvinist pigs. This country got what it deserved."

Boone tried to control his anger. "Well, I'm an American, and so are you. If you want to go to Canada, it's a free country."

We ate our food, then pissed in a field and hit the road again. With the sun high in the sky, it was easy to spot road kill: an arm here, a leg there, a trunk with a wide tire mark set deep in its ribs, and finally a head, its jaws still moving. All human, all ghoulish. Rotting guts covered the pavement and blood congealed in cool sunlight. Some semi-truck driver must have had a field day.

In Colorado, we found a truck tipped over on the side of the road, the meatless remains of its driver a dozen feet away, an empty revolver at his side. Boone opened the cargo doors and we gazed at cases of Slim Jim meat sticks, Hostess Twinkies, canned energy drinks, and bottled water.

"Too bad we can't roll this bad boy over," Boone said. "We'd never starve."

We packed all the supplies we could.

"I'm so happy to get out of that fucking town," Marion said. "Materialistic motherfuckers. The goddamned world is ending, and all they want to do is force their capitalist agenda on the rest of the survivors. I wish to God we'd had time to open the gates in their fascist little community and allow the ghouls inside. That would have leveled the playing field between the haves and the have-nots."

"Didn't you grow up there?" I said.

"Yeah, and my parents are as bad as the rest of them. I hope they all get eaten. It would serve them right: they've been cannibalizing society their whole lives."

I wondered what we had gotten ourselves into now.

We found a little ranch house with a FOR SALE sign its overgrown front lawn. We had to break a window to get in. The house was empty and clean, and we hid our bikes in the garage. Then we removed a closet door and secured it against the window we had broken. Sitting on a carpeted floor, we ate our chips, meat sticks and Twinkies, and washed them down with water.

"We've got to start all over," Marion said. "Only this time, we have to do things right."

"You sound just like those teabaggers," Boone said.

"Fuck you, how can I sound like them? I'm talking about the opposite of their philosophy: no ownership, no moneyed elections, no power trips for people just because they were born with a silver spoon in their mouth. It's time for regular, working people to have an equal say and equal stake in how the world is run."

Boone's nostrils flared, so I stood and looked at Marion.

"Why don't we go check out the rest of the house?" I said.

Her eyes met mine. "Okay."

We found a bedroom and closed the door, and in seconds our hands groped each other, undoing buttons and belts, pulling zippers, tugging at denim. She was hot and wet, and I was hard, so I guess we fit together pretty well. I didn't bother to use a rubber, and she didn't bother to hold out because of it; she gave as good as she got, and when we groaned at the same time and lay panting and sweating on the carpet, I thought maybe we stood a chance. Then she started talking, so I fucked her again to shut her up. It went on like that most of the night.

In the morning, we ate Slim Jims and potato chips for breakfast and washed them down with energy drinks. I enjoyed the day's ride because I didn't have to listen to Marion's political crap. But when we ate lunch at a campsite overlooking a ravine she started up again.

"If women were in charge, this never would have happened. You just know these ghouls are the result of some military experiment gone wrong, don't you? Blame that on men."

"Mayor Bachlin was a woman," Boone said. "You didn't think much of her."

Oh, God. Don't encourage her.

"That's because Bachlin's playing a man's game. She's no feminist: she wears her hair and her make-up the way she does, and stays in shape, and plays those guys for the fools they are. She wraps her husband around her finger and screws the sheriff, and who knows who else, and the men just eat it up. You're all idiots, thinking with your little heads instead of your big heads. You'll do anything for a little pussy, won't you?"

When it was time to go, I sat on my bike and used one hand to prevent Marion from doing the same.

"What's going on?" she said.

"It's the end of the road for you."

"What are you talking about? We had a deal."

"I never agreed to anything. I couldn't, because you never let me get a word in edgewise. This trip's over for you."

"But I let you fuck me!"

"You enjoyed that as much as I did, and we both feel better because of it. Now it's time to say goodbye."

Spittle flew from her mouth, which wasn't very attractive. "You used me. You only wanted one thing!"

"If you mean I only wanted to shut you up for five minutes, you got that right."

She looked around the campsite, her tits rising and falling. "You can't just leave me here! I'll never make it."

"You're a strong woman, I'm sure you'll get by."

With her eyes wide, Marion ran over to Boone.

"What about you? We're closer to the same age anyway."

Smiling, Boone shrugged. "Sorry. Do you think I want to go where he's been?"

She looked from him to me. "You're both bastards. Pigs, like all men!"

I started my engine.

"At least give me a gun and some food."

"You'd only shoot us in the back." I opened my throttle and took off.

"You motherfucking assholes! You're both queer! I hate you!"

I only drove about two hundred yards before I stopped. When Boone pulled up beside me, I got off my bike and walked to the trailer. I took out my M-16, waved it in the air, then tossed it on the ground. Then I took out what I estimated to be one third of the Slim Jims, potato chips, Twinkies, energy drinks, and bottled water, and set them on the ground too.

Marion walked toward us, her tear stricken face twisted with rage. I blew her a kiss and we drove off. I'm no choir boy.

There are stars in every city,
In every house and on every street,
And if you walk down Hollywood Boulevard
Their names are written in concrete!

The Kinks, "Celluloid Heroes"

2

The ghouls in Utah irritated us as much as the living Mormons did.

The drive through Nevada unsettled me. I was grateful for the heat—fuck you, Buffalo!—until we drove through the desert. I took a piss and my urine evaporated as it splashed the sun-baked clay. You know you've reached hell when you see I saw two buzzards feeding on a ghoul staggering along the road.

In California, we spent a week getting drunk at an abandoned winery. The property wasn't fenced in, and the ghouls found us. Most of them were Mexicans, and we reasoned that they had toiled in the vineyards long enough that they deserved the run of the place, so we let them have it. It was nice while it lasted, but I've always preferred beer to wine anyway.

The drive along the coast was treacherous and fun.

With all the abandoned cars on the highway, we never had a problem finding gas. The problem we had was the ghouls: we saw thousands of them, maybe hundreds of thousands. Dead cops, dead gang members, dead teenagers, dead bikers, dead firemen, dead National Guards... I felt like we'd crossed into another country, one occupied solely by the dead. Wildfires burned in the hills and coyotes and cougars roamed free in the suburbs. Driving on the freeway was like running an obstacle course, so many dead people walked the asphalt. It became exhausting. America was a dead country, a nation of the dead, and I found myself wondering how things were up in Canada.

The Hollywood sign overlooked the smog-embalmed city below like the epitaph on a giant gravestone. We stood beneath its letters, which looked ratty up close, and studied the city. Burning buildings coughed up black smoke which merged with the smog. Hollywood didn't look any more glamorous than Buffalo.

"You sure you want to go down there?" I said.

Boone seemed uncertain. "We came all this way..."

We ate our last Slim Jims and washed them down with water because we'd finished the energy drinks, then drove into Hollywood, home of the stars. The sidewalks were crowded with ghoul hookers, ghoul roller bladers that had lost the knack, ghoul drug addicts and dealers and pimps, and ghoul teenagers.

Ghouls! Ghouls! Ghouls!

We wove between the walking corpses, and before long we came upon Grauman's Chinese Theater, a pillar of tackiness in a tacky city that now belonged to the dead. Staring at the residents, I wondered how many of them had traveled here with stars in their eyes and had sold their souls for nothing and remained only because there was no returning home. How many had become undead even before they died and revived? There were no longer any beautiful people in Hollywood, if there ever had been.

Boone pulled ahead of me and stood. "Look!"

I followed his finger to the ghouls meandering along the Hollywood Walk of Fame. Hundreds of them shambled from side to side there, maybe a thousand. I looked closer at a ghoul in mini skirt who looked almost medicated. It was—or had been—Paula Abdul. Then Brad Pitt shambled by, an unlit cigarette in one hand. Corey Feldman appeared lost. Lindsey Lohan looked the same. Winona Ryder looked better. Justin Bieber had gained a personality. One of the Kardashian sisters was nude from head to toe, her body bloated and purple. Al Pacino's hair had grown out, long and white with six inches of dyed black at the ends. I couldn't tell if Teri Hatcher's face looked tight because she was dead, or because her plastic surgery had collapsed. Faces sagged as badly as tits; no amount of makeup, Botox, or silicone would restore their former luster. One of the broads from *Sex and the City* staggered toward us. I raised my .45 and she stopped and looked at me, then turned away. I let her go; unable to speak, she no longer annoyed me.

"Why aren't they trying to eat us?" Boone said.

"They spent their lives trying to get their stars on the Walk of Fame. Now they don't want to leave it. Or maybe they're waiting for us to ask for their autographs."

Gary Dugan turned in our direction, his face mottled and gray, and Boone burst into laughter. Behind us, a hundred non-celebrity ghouls shambled toward us.

"Seen enough?" I said.

"Yeah, that was cool."

And that was that.

Up in the hills, we finished our potato chips and Twinkies. At least we still had water.

"Where do you want to go next?" Boone said.

"How about Canada?"

"Canada's cold. Don't you like this weather?"

"Not enough to share it with ten million ghouls. We seem to be the only snack in town."

"I don't want to go to Canada. Their TV shows suck."

"There are no more TV shows."

"They talk funny. Let's go to Texas instead."

"They don't talk funny in Texas?"

"When someone in Texas talks funny they sound cool, like J.R. Ewing on *Dallas*."

So we set off for Texas.

In Arizona, the highway was so cluttered with abandoned vehicles that we had to get off the road just to pass them, which proved difficult for Boone. We had all the gas we wanted and we started checking cages for food and other supplies. In plenty of instances, entire families of ghouls sat trapped in their vehicles, trying to figure a way out. I saw an overweight female ghoul sitting behind the wheel of her SUV with a cell phone pressed against her ear. In the trunk of a Firebird, we hit payday: two boxes of ramen noodles, one beef and the other chicken. As I loaded the noodles into my saddle bags, a shadow fell over me. My body stiffened, and Boone's M-16 issued a single round. The shadow fell away and I gave it no thought.

A few hours later we sat at a picnic table in a rest area eating our noodles, which we had cooked over an open fire. An armed militia of about twenty men passed us on foot, carrying rifles. I thought about all the crazy stories I'd heard about Arizona, and my spine stiffened. Fortunately, they were just ghouls and when they turned toward us we reduced their brains to pumpkin mush.

I'm not one for sleeping under the open stars when there are cannibalistic creatures about, so on the New Mexico border we rolled our bikes inside a rest stop with a food court and barricaded the front doors with vending machines. The place had been stripped bare, and the corpses of several ghouls littered the floor. We did a pretty thorough check with our flashlights, but I wasn't entirely satisfied, so we rolled my bike into the men's room and slept in there. Boone was pissed that his chopper didn't fit and we had to leave it in the dining area, but that's what happens when you ride on three wheels instead of two.

Lying on that floor, I wondered how Marion was doing. Hell, I even wondered how Mayor Bachlin was doing. With the human race the minority group among bipeds, we needed to stick together, but the same old differences kept us apart: sexual politics and politics of power. It must have been November already.

We rode into Texas in the morning, and I was impressed by the expansive oil fields and cattle ranches. Hours passed before we saw any ghouls, and we never did see any people that first day. But we sure saw a lot of cows. Around 2:00 p.m. I pulled over to the side of the road and Boone followed suit.

"Are you thinking what I am?" I said.

"Hell, yeah."

We parked our bikes, armed ourselves, and crossed the long field. I caught a whiff of the beasts, which took some getting used to. The cows looked well fed, which I guess was no surprise: there was no shortage of grass, after all. We walked alongside the beasts and I estimated there were at least fifty head of cattle just standing there. I don't know the proper way to choose livestock for dinner, but we finally found a cow we agreed on. I raised my rifle and fired a round into the beast's brain, dropping it. The herd stampeded in the other direction, kicking up a cloud of dust that was something to behold. Yee-haw.

I gestured at my kill. "Skin it, bitch."

Boone raised his eyebrows. "How do you figure?"

"I killed it. You cook it."

"You'll build the fire?"

"Deal."

Drawing his hunting knife, Boone stepped forward. "Good luck finding firewood."

It took hours to cook the beef, but it was worth the time. The meat was a little tough on the outside and a little rare on the inside, but we had no complaints.

"How's your arm?" Boone said.

I showed him my sore limb, which had grown even more discolored. "Hurts like hell. I guess it's infected."

Boone's expression showed concern. "You think I need to cut it off?"

"With what, that hunting knife of yours? No thanks."

"I'm serious. It might become necessary."

"How the hell do you think I'm going to ride my bike with one arm?"

He chewed his beef. "I guess you'll ride behind me. Then you'll be my bitch."

"Fuck you, junior."

"Hey, I missed my chance with Marion. You're all I've got left."

I aimed my fork at him. "I aim to outlive you."

"I'm glad to hear it." Rising, he scanned the horizon in each direction. "There's still no sign of them."

"They're somewhere. This is a big state."

"Don't mess with Texas."

We found what amounted to little more than a shack for shelter. It didn't even have a door, but at least it had four walls and a roof, so I parked my bike in the empty doorway. We had no way to refrigerate the beef, so we bought a big chunk with us and ate another meal before going to bed. The wind howled outside, but at least it didn't rain. When the sun rose, we looked around and saw no ghouls. We cooked ramen noodles for breakfast, then set off. I had a bad feeling in my stomach that once he'd had his fill of Texas, Boone intended to rope me into going to Florida. That was probably his whole plan all along; ever the contrarian, he couldn't have just agreed to Florida when I suggested it, he had to take the long way there.

We kept on truckin' until I heard Boone honking his horn. When I checked my rearview mirror I didn't see him, so I slowed down and turned around. I'd left him in my dust almost a quarter of a mile behind me. When I caught up to him he was hunched over his gas tank, and a sick feeling grew in the pit of my stomach. With a frown on his face he looked at me and shook his head.

Fuck.

"Don't we have gas in the trailer?"

He shook his head and my temples throbbed.

"I guess you'll have to share."

I looked at my fuel gauge, then at the horizon. "I've only got an eighth of a tank left. I could have sworn we had another tank..."

"What the hell are we going to do?"

I looked at a nearby road sign. "I guess we're going to San Antonio. You ride with me and we'll come back for your chopper."

"Shit!" Boone kicked up dust. He looked at the sign. "'Population 2,000,000.' We're so fucked."

"Get that empty can, unless you plan to bring the gas back in your mouth."

He fetched the can and the rest of our ammo, and we packed my saddle bags full. Then he climbed on my bike and locked his hands around my sternum.

"Bitch," I said.

San Antonio was a hell of a city. We saw plenty of broken windows, but at least none of the buildings were burning. An occasional ghoul lumbered in the street, but not enough to cause us alarm. We found a shiny black pickup and siphoned its gas, filling my tank as well as the gas can. Everything was going to be okay.

For some reason I obeyed the traffic signs, circling the city block to avoid going the wrong way on a one-way street, and I hit the brakes hard as Boone screamed in my ear. Half a block ahead of us, two hundred ghouls moved in our direction, scores of dead eyes shaded by ten-gallon hats. With my heart pounding I made a right hand turn and ran straight into another wall of undead flesh. I didn't even slow down, I just made a left hand turn to escape and we found ourselves facing another legion of ghouls. There were so many of them! Unlike the ghouls who had fled the cities in Kansas to find food, those in Texas had gravitated toward this city for the same reason. I cut through an alley, and we rode straight through the first crowd we encountered. Boone did better brushing them aside with the butt of his M-16 than shooting them. I sped through the outstretched limbs and fingers, gunning my hog's engine.

Somehow, we found ourselves in another crowd of ghouls, this one occupying an open plaza. I steered around one ghoul, drove into another, and rode over another one after that. Filthy fingers clawed at my face and hair, and I had no choice but to slow down. The damned things were everywhere, all around us. Boone screamed as one of them pulled him off my backseat. Death overwhelmed me.

Shots fired from several guns, and heads exploded around me. I raced forward, unable to see beyond the hungry dead things directly in front of me, while my unseen saviors continued to fire. I found myself facing two massive wooden doors, and I heard Boone's screams behind me. As dead hands continued to claw at me, I turned my bike around and rode it straight into the ghouls, running over as many of them as possible.

Seven of the damned things stood hunched over something, and I knew that something had to be my partner. I jerked my Savage 110 free of its holster and opened fire. At the same time, I heard gunshots somewhere above me, and blood and chunks of flesh struck me from behind. When I ran out of ammo I slammed the rifle back in its holster and pulled my .45 from its holster. I rode deeper into the ghouls and popped three of them in the head. They slumped forward and Boone pushed them off him. He was in bad shape: a chunk of flesh had been torn out of his neck, and bite wounds covered both of his arms, candy colored blood glistening. His eyes were wild with panic. I reached down and he grasped my arm, and I pulled him back onto my bike while gunshots rang out around us. Shambling bodies continued to crowd us. I searched the ground for Boone's M-16 but the damned thing was nowhere to be found. A ghoul bit my arm, but my MC saved my hide. I shot the cowboy in the forehead, then opened fire on the crowd. The first shots drove the ghouls back, then I went for their heads. I dropped three of them, but another three took their places.

When the gun clicked in my hands, I discarded it and pulled the Colt free of my boot. I knew that fucker would come in handy. I fired straight ahead, clearing a path as I drove forward. Boone screamed in my ear, and other gunshots tore into the ghouls standing between us and the double doors. The bodies piled up so high that I couldn't get over them anymore, so I took the only chance we had: I hit the brakes, hopped off my hog, grabbed Boone, and slung him over my shoulders. I didn't just abandon my bike, I abandoned my rifle and all the ammo in my saddle bags. With Boone's weigh holding me down, I staggered toward the doors, praying they would open.

They did, and that's how we ended up in the Alamo.

Hey Santa Anna, we're killing your soldiers below!
That men wherever they go, will remember the Alamo...

Johnny Cash, "Remember the Alamo"

1

I fell through the doors and into a crowd of people and landed on the ground with Boone atop me. A few gunshots rang out and Boone cried out as the doors closed behind us. He rolled over my head with a pained groan and hands helped me to my feet. Maybe one hundred faces stared at me belonging to men, women and children. Some wore cowboy hats, others coonskin caps. Upon closer inspection, I realized the caps were made of imitation fur, and purchased—or looted—from a souvenir store.

"Welcome to the Alamo," a big man said.

"Thanks."

Two men and a woman helped Boone to his feet. Blood flowed from the bite wounds on his body.

"Get him up to the infirmary," the big man said.

The woman and one of the men escorted Boone through the crowd and up a narrow flight of stairs. A walkway surrounded the clay mission, and a dozen men with rifles stood upon it, facing in all directions: my heroes.

"Goddamn if that wasn't the goddamnedest thing I've ever seen," the big man said. "You got some set of balls on you, going after a man who's been bitten."

"He's not just any man; he's my friend."

"Pards, huh? Well, what brings you boys to San Antonio?"

I thought about it. "I'm not sure. A whim, I guess."

He slapped my back. "You always had such bad hunches?"

Around me people roared.

"I'm glad to be here with you folks just the same."

"You think so? I appreciate the sentiment. We all do. It's good to be in agreeable company, especially seeing as how we're all going to die together."

I looked at the people staring at me. Their expressions showed resignation, defeat, and something else I couldn't put my finger on.

"Where are you from, friend?"

"Buffalo."

"Buffalo?" He guffawed. "Why the hell didn't you go to Canada? Before everything went dark they had everything under control over there. Last I heard, their biggest problem was dealing with all the Americans sneaking over the border illegally!"

Great, I thought as laughter enveloped me from every direction. "Can I get something to drink?"

"You came to the wrong place for that. We haven't had water in two days, or food in five. We're all dehydrated and operating on empty stomachs. We're as hungry as those sorry sons of bitches outside, and it's pretty damned certain that they're going to eat before any of us do, unless we start eating each other. Come on, let me show you something."

He led me to a ladder, which we climbed to the gangway. We were only on the second floor, but I could see all the way up the street. Only I couldn't see the street, any of it, because thousands of ghouls, more than any I had ever seen before, filled the plaza and the surrounding streets. The big Texan led me around the perimeter of the mission-turned-fort-turned-tourist-trap-turned-fort again. From every vantage point, ghouls stretching as far as I could see, their moans carried on the wind; it was the million dead man march, the biggest zombie crawl the world had ever seen. Up here, the stench was overwhelming.

"You see our predicament. There's no way out, no allowing the women and children to leave before the pending massacre. We're out of food and water, and we're just about out of ammo. We keep reinforcing the doors, but there's so many of those damned things out there that it's just a matter of time before their sheer combined weight busts them down. We're sitting ducks."

I got the picture. "I've got ammo in the saddlebags of my bike."

"Ammo for what?"

"An M-16, mostly."

"We ain't got any M-16s, do you?"

"Somewhere... out there."

"Shoot, we'd have to waste the last of the ammo that we have providing cover for you to run out there and try to retrieve what you left behind. That's a fool's mission, with no likely return on our investment."

I knew he was right. "I'd like to see my friend."

"Sure you would." He led me to the infirmary and held out his hand. "My name's Fullerton."

I shook his outstretched paw. "Walker."

"Good to know you."

"Same here."

He walked away and I entered the infirmary, which was nothing more than a room crowded with too many occupied cots. Boone was one of six people lying down. His wounds had been dressed, and two women acting as nurses hovered nearby. Even though Boone mustered a smile, he reminded me of Deke on his deathbed.

"You still here? I thought you'd have run out by now."

I stood at his bedside. "I would if I could. Looks like we're stuck with each other."

He grimaced. "So I hear. We'd have been better off with those teabaggers in Kansas."

"I'd rather 'Live Free or Die.'"

Boone snorted. "Yeah, we should have gone to New Hampshire."

"We should have gone to Canada. I hear everything's dandy there."

"Rub it in. Now I won't see Florida again before I die."

"I knew it."

"Well, why didn't you say something then? You should have talked me out of this road trip, or gone your own way. At least one of us might have made it."

I shrugged. "What would I have done my own, except relax in peace and quiet?"

"Shit, you'd have died have boredom. You need someone around to do enough talking for two."

"Well, you more than fit that bill, don't you?"

"It's not like I had much of a choice. A grown man with nothing to say, I swear." He sighed. "I wish I had a joint."

"We're going to starve to death and you want to get stoned? This is not a good time to have the munchies."

"I'm in pain, okay? Besides, we had ourselves a hell of a last meal. I'd like a last toke as well, do you mind?"

I lowered my voice. "There's a lot of those things out there; half the state of Texas, by the look of it. They'll get in here before we can starve."

"But maybe not before I croak and rise. I suppose you left all our guns out there."

"Well I didn't have much choice, did I? It was you or the guns. But I kept my Colt, and I saved one bullet."

He swallowed. "Just one?"

"I'm afraid so."

"You promised me..."

"Goddamn, but you're selfish! I don't know how I put up with your whining for so long."

"You're just saying that because you're going to miss me."

"Maybe."

"It's okay. I'll miss you too."

I wanted to clasp his shoulder but I knew that would only aggravate his wounds.

"But I'm still holding you to your promise."

"Oh, for God's sake!" I made a show out of storming out of the infirmary, but I just wanted to get away so I could wipe the tears forming in my eyes. I really was going to miss the little cocksucker, and I hated to see him deteriorating.

I trotted down the stairs and walked around the compound. A guy who stood even taller than me, who wore tight black jeans, a tight black T-shirt, and a black cowboy hat on his head, used chalk to write a manifesto on one clay wall. He had a thick black mustache but no sideburns, and I knew he wore the macho cowboy hat to cover a bald head. I stared at his handiwork.

"What are you writing?" I said.

"The truth. Christ, I miss my blog."

"What's the truth?"

"That liberals caused the end of the world."

"I thought the ghouls did that."

"The ghouls are just a symptom. The liberals are the cause. It's their fault we're in this position. It's all a communist plot. Or the Muslims."

Unbelievable: he wanted to continue the same old debates right until the end. "What difference does it really make now?"

He looked at me for the first time. "It makes a world of difference. Someone's got to know what happened here."

"Like who?"

"I don't know; the marines, maybe. Or the cavalry. Or space aliens. Someone's going to come here, after all of this is over, and they need to know what happened to us, why we fell from grace."

At least when he was busy writing he wasn't talking. "Good luck."

Making my way through the crowd, I climbed a ladder to the gangway and looked out at the undead army desperate to get inside. They didn't want to conquer us, they just wanted to eat us.

"What's your name, mister?"

Turning, I faced a little girl with brown hair and a smudged face. "Walker."

"No, I mean your *first* name."

I thought about it. For years, I'd only ever used my first name in court. "Jim. What's yours?"

"Molly," she said.

"That's a pretty name. How old are you?"

"Nine."

"Where are your parents?"

She nodded at the ghouls outside. "Out there somewhere. They tried to eat me."

I didn't know what to say to that. "Who are you here with?"

"Nobody. My aunt brought me here, but she died. They put a bullet in her brain so she wouldn't come back, and they threw her over the edge. The other ghouls ate her."

A little girl shouldn't have such a firm grasp of the way the world works. "Isn't anyone watching over you now?"

She shook her head. "I have a friend. Her name is Sarah, and she's ten. But her parents don't want us to play together anymore. They want to spend together as a family now that the end is here. There's no food, and those ghouls will be coming in soon."

The kid broke my heart. "I know."

"Do you have any kids?"

"I have a son, somewhere." Maybe. "But he's all grown up. He doesn't need me to take care of him."

"Everyone needs somebody."

"You're right. Hey, I've got an idea: how about if we watch out for each other? We can be friends."

"You came here with another man, I saw you. Isn't he your friend?"

"Yes, he is. But you can never have too many friends, so how about it?"

She gave me an enthusiastic nod. I held out my hand, which she shook. Her flesh felt soft, and I knew it would tear easily when the ghouls got their hands on her. She threw her arms around my legs, so I got down on one knee and held her. She sobbed in my arms, and I rocked her back and forth.

"It's okay, honey. You cry all you want."

But she stopped after a while.

"Hey, would you like to meet my friend? His name's Boone."

"Like Daniel Boone?"

I laughed. "Sure, like Daniel Boone."

"I like Davy Crockett better, but okay."

I took her hand. "Come on."

When we entered the infirmary, Boone winced with pain.

"Well, aren't you full of surprises?" he said.

I pulled a chair over to the side of his bed and sat on it, then set the girl on my lap. "This is Molly. I asked her to keep me company."

Boone offered Molly a pained smile. "Pleased to meet you. Good luck getting him to say anything interesting."

"I like him," Molly said.

"That's because you're too young to know better."

"Don't listen to him," I said. "He was born ornery."

Boone drew in his breath and let out a series of short gasps. "They tell me Colonel Travis died up here. Remember him?"

"The guy who drew the line in the sand with his sword?"

"Yeah, Laurence Harvey played him in the John Wayne movie. They gave him two flintlock pistols when he was dying and he took out a bunch of Mexicans when they came in. I wish I had two pistols."

"They'd be wasted on you. You never could hit anything until you got your hands on that M-16."

"I saved your ass with more guns than I can remember." Pain seized control of his face, sweat forming. He nodded at Molly. "She's asleep."

I looked down at her. She had bowed her head against my chest.

"I suppose you're going to tell me you found a better use for that bullet you saved."

I shrugged. "Do you disagree?"

He shook his head. "Boy, I'll tell you. Some people…" He looked at me. "I don't want to come back as one of those things."

"Then hang on and don't die. When they get in here, they're not going to leave anything left of any of us. There's thousands of them out there, they're going to pick our bones clean." I glanced at Molly. "When the time comes, I'll make sure she doesn't suffer. Then me and you can go down at the same time."

"You make it sound so cozy. I've already been bitten, and I can tell you it hurts like hell. I just want it to be over."

I reached out and took his hand. "It won't be long now."

"We should have gone to Canada."

"Big of you to say."

"You forgive me?"

"Hell, there's nothing to forgive. What are friends for?"

He closed his eyes and slept. I took my journal out of my jacket pocket and got caught up on the day's events with Molly asleep on my lap. There's nothing left to do now but wait.

THE AUTHOR

As an adolescent, Gregory Lamberson feared a thumbnail picture of arthritic hands clawing through a boarded up window in the back pages of *Famous Monsters of Filmland*. This iconic image was the cover for John Russo's novelization of *Night of the Living Dead*, and young Lamberson eventually bought the cheap paperback. Despite an abiding love for monsters, he knew he was not emotionally equipped to deal with flesh-eating ghouls. But when he was twelve years old, he convinced a liberal-minded uncle to take him to see the George Romero film at a repertory theater in Washington, D.C., which proved to be the most terrifying and eye-opening experience of his prepubescent life.

"Uncle Bill" later took Lamberson to see the Romero films *Dawn of the Dead* and *Martin* during their original theatrical runs, and the aspiring horrormeister studied filmmaking at New York City's School of Visual Arts specifically because one of its instructors, Roy Frumkes, directed the feature-length *Document of the Dead* with an SVA student crew. Although Lamberson has directed four feature films, including the cult classic *Slime City* and its recent sequel *Slime City Massacre*, and has written several horror novels, including *Personal Demons*, *Johnny Gruesome*, and *The Frenzy Way*, and has dealt with voodoo zombies in *Desperate Souls* and the upcoming *Tortured Spirits*, he has never ventured into the world of flesh-eaters created by Russo and Romero until now. It's a bleak place, and he wouldn't want to live there; still, there may yet be stories of Boone and Walker to be written.

Visit Lamberson at www.slimeguy.com, or on Facebook or Twitter.

COMING SOON FROM PRINT IS DEAD

PALE PREACHERS
TOM PICCIRILLI

VESPERS
TOM PICCIRILLI

THE SLABS
NATE SOUTHARD

THEM BONES
ROBERT N. LEE

THE LIVING
**KEALAN PATRICK BURKE
& RJ SEVIN**

1974.

The Summer of Love is a fading memory, the Cold War rages on, Richard M. Nixon is barely holding onto the Presidency, and the dead are returning to life.

Five friends on their way to a week at Lake Tahoe, a Vietnam veteran in Sacramento trying to get home to his daughter in New Mexico, an older couple idling in a dusty shop in the hills, and a dangerous man who has spent twenty years preparing his strange family for the end of the world...

As civilization collapses, these scattered survivors cross paths, and the hungry dead are the least of the horrors unleashed.

Those who die will walk. Those who live will hope for a quick death, and they will...

PRAY TO STAY DEAD

a new experiment in terror by
MASON JAMES COLE

"A brutally entertaining collision of zombie thriller and grindhouse action. Not for the faint of heart!"

Jonathan Maberry, *New York Times* bestselling author of *Patient Zero*

"[A] revelation, one of those books that reminds you why you liked the genre in the first place.... Buy it, buy it, buy it."

Badass Digest

MILLWOOD WAS A GOOD PLACE TO BE WHEN THE DEAD ROSE.

Small, isolated, easy to defend. The survivors there forged a community, weathered what came, and began to prosper.

But then they ran out of food.

Now, Millwood is sending five men to the neighboring town of Rundberg, a place ruled by three thousand living dead, to find enough food to save their community.

Five against three thousand?

...they don't stand a chance.

"Nate Southard's *Scavengers* has got everything fans of the zombie genre crave: huge cannibalistic crowds of the undead, violent, almost continuous action, mounting paranoia and dread... Not since Richard Matheson have we had a writer so adept at dangling the average American guy on the end of a rope so we can watch him twitch and turn in the wind."

Joe McKinney, **author of *Dead City***

NATE SOUTHARD

SCAVENGERS

THERE ARE NO RULES

WORLD IN RED

A ZOMBIE NOVEL

JOHN SEBASTIAN GORUMBA

"This is how it's done, folks. This is how you tell a horror story in the 21st century... I can't wait to see where Gorumba goes from here, because this guy knows how to deliver the scares."

Joe McKinney, author of *Dead City*
and *Apocalypse of the Dead*

"...[T]he most relentlessly bleak novel I've read since *The Road*."

Alex Riviello, *Badass Digest*

reanimated americans

Martin Mundt

With **Reanimated Americans**, author Martin Mundt has created a malignant masterpiece. Like a literary mad scientist armed with diabolical narrative skill and a mordant sense of humor, Mundt manages to mash up the zombie mythos with both mayhem and Swiftian satire. **Reanimated Americans** is a must-read for undead-heads of all persuasions, slithering from laugh-out-loud sequences to gut-wrenching gore with the greatest of ease. **Highly recommended!**

Jay Bonansinga, National Bestselling author of *Perfect Victim, Pinkerton's War* and co-author of *The Walking Dead: Rise Of The Governor*

Jett Ahrens has just joined the Zombie Division of the Census Bureau, hoping for a dull, uncomplicated job counting the country's newest citizens—the Living Dead. Y'know: Zombies, Rotters, Grave Potatoes, but don't call them any of those names. They're Reanimated Americans, and they aren't anything like their cinematic counterparts—they don't eat your flesh or want your brains. They just… stand around. Loitering. Stinking up the place.

Easy enough, yeah, but one of Jett's partners might be a little nuts, and then there's the serial re-killer going around town and setting walking dead folks on fire. Not to mention the Red Death Gang transforming the undead into works of art. Or the pair of psychotic cops tracking the serial re-killer and wreaking havoc of their own.

Or the nasty secret Jett keeps in a rental storage unit…

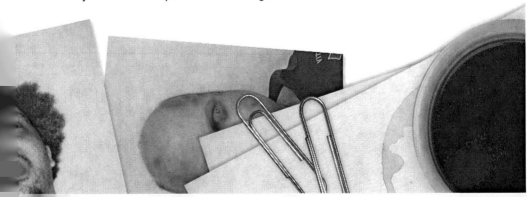

JOE McKINNEY

DATING *in* DEAD WORLD

The Collected Zombie Stories, Volume I

SUMMER 2012

AMERICA IS DIVIDED.

A massive wall has been constructed to separate Free America, where life is as normal as it ever was, from the regions of Texas and the Gulf Coast populated by millions of the flesh-eating dead and the hopeless survivors they hunt—the so-called Forgotten. With so much desperate hunger, the equilibrium afforded by the wall can not hold, and there are rumors of a secret passage from the Quarantine Zone into Free America.

Investigative journalist Samantha Calloway isn't satisfied with a rumor, nor with an entire segment of U.S. citizenry being forgotten. One night, in search of answers, she steals past the Coast Guard blockade and lands on a deserted beach in South Texas. Her mission: spend three weeks wandering the ruins, finding out how those left behind live their lives and whether or not escape is possible. Get in and get out. It's all supposed to be very easy.

But in the Quarantine Zone, every scrap, morsel, and movement has a price, and the only thing that comes easy is death.

Set in Joe McKinney's Dead World (*Dead City, Apocalypse of the Dead, Flesh Eaters,* and the upcoming *Mutated*), *The Crossing* sets the stage for his epic zombie collection, *Dating in Dead World: The Collected Zombie Stories, Volume One*, coming from Print Is Dead Books in Summer 2012.

Includes a four-chapter extended preview of *Scavengers* by Nate Southard.

THE CROSSING
JOE McKINNEY

"A rising star on the horror scene."
Fearnet.com

CAN'T GET ENOUGH
GREGORY LAMBERSON?

Check out these acclaimed,
pulse-racing titles from Medallion Press.

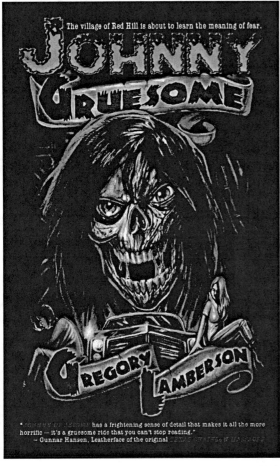

The village of Red Hill is about to learn the meaning of fear.

JOHNNY GRUESOME

GREGORY LAMBERSON

"JOHNNY GRUESOME has a frightening sense of detail that makes it all the more horrific — it's a gruesome ride that you can't stop reading."
— Gunnar Hansen, Leatherface of the original TEXAS CHAINSAW MASSACRE

The upstate village of Red Hill is about to learn the meaning of fear.

Johnny Grissom, nicknamed "Johnny Gruesome" by his high school classmates, is a heavy-metal hellion who loves to party, watch horror movies, and get into fights. His best friend, Eric, admires him, and his girlfriend, Karen, loves him.

One winter night, Johnny's car, the Death Mobile, is discovered submerged beneath the icy surface of Willow Creekt, with Johnny's water-logged corpse inside. The residents of Red Hill believe that Johnny's death was accidental.

Then the murders begin—horrible acts of violent vengeance that hint at a deepening mystery and terror yet to come. A headless body is discovered at the high school. A priest is forced to confront his own misdeeds. And a mortician encounters the impossible.

One by one, Johnny's enemies meet a grisly demise, as the sound of a car engine and maniacal laughter fill the night. The students at Red Hill High School fear for their lives—especially Johnny's closest friends, who harbor a dark secret.

If people thought Johnny had a bad attitude when he was alive, wait until they encounter him when he's dead!

Johnny Gruesome is a valentine to E.C. Comics, Marvel's *Tomb of Dracula*, and such gory 1980s splatter flicks as *I* and *Return of the Living Dead*. The novel is a horror fan's nightmare come true!

MEDALLION
P R E S S
MEDALLIONMEDIAGROUP.COM

AVAILABLE IN PRINT
AND E-BOOK FORMATS

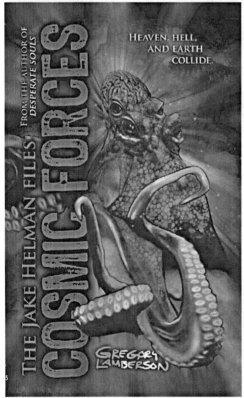

THE
JAKE HELMAN FILES

Jake Helman, New York homicide detective turned private eye, risks his very sou to battle supernatural forces in this heart-pounding series, which includes *Persona Demons, Desperate Souls, and Cosmic Forces*

AVAILABLE IN PRINT
AND E-BOOK FORMATS

MEDALLION
P R E S S
MEDALLIONMEDIAGROUI

THE FRENZY CYCLE

Police procedural and bloody werewolf action mingle in this razor-sharp series, which includes *The Frenzy Way* and *The Frenzy War*.

MEDALLION
PRESS

Slime City Massacre written and directed by Gregory Lamberson

Slime City Massacre takes place seven years in the future, after a dirty bomb has decimated New York City's financial district and reduced midtown to a post-apocalyptic nightmare . . . *Slime City*. Into this hostile environment arrive Alexa (Jennifer Bihl) and Cory (Kealan Patrick Burke), a draft dodger and an Army deserter hoping to find refuge. In a seemingly deserted building, they encounter Mason (Lee Perkins) and Alice (Debbie Rochon), two hardened survivors who teach them the ropes. In flashbacks, we see how Zachary Devon (Robert C. Sabin, star of *Slime City*) indoctrinates a prostitute named Nicole (Brooke Lewis) in his "Coven of Flesh," and we learn why he and his followers committed mass suicide. When Alexa, Cory, Mason, and Alice discover Zachary's "home-brewed elixir" and "Himalayan yogurt" in the ruins of his soup kitchen, all four characters are possessed by the spirits of Zachary and his followers, with outrageous results. Throw in homeless people, mercenaries, and mutant cannibals, and you have the recipe for an epic battle: the *Slime City Massacre*.

If you'd like to check out everything the Slime Guy, Gregory Lamberson, is up to, visit him at his site: www.slimeguy.com. He's a man well worth keeping up with!

MEDALLION
MEDIA GROUP
MEDALLIONMEDIAGROUP.COM

CPSIA information can be obtained at www.ICGtesting.com
Printed in the USA
LVOW130045130613

338189LV00005B/868/P